# LOWER WORLD

## MAYA DANIELS

BOOKS

## By Maya Daniels

Infernal Regions for the Unprepared

*Black Hand*

*Lower World*

*Everlasting Fire*

*Place of Torment*

Vinci Books

vinci-books.com

Published by Vinci Books Ltd in 2025

1

A CIP catalogue record for this book is available from the British Library.
Paperback ISBN: 9781036706609

# Chapter One

"Sooo ... do I add Mistress at the end of what I'm saying because you're a girl and I can't say Sire to you? Or do I need to say Mistress first before any other word is spoken?"

Alice leaned forward, gripping the recliner tightly on both sides of her legs while staring so intently I truly believed she was trying to use telepathy to force me to tell her the truth. I watched in fascination as the thick frames of her glasses started sliding down her nose. She's been like this ever since we did that horrible ritual to try and remove the cursed pendant that was stuck around my neck. I was desperate to have it gone at the time, unlike now when I knew better. Regardless of my feelings about it, my human friend was convinced more than ever that she was a witch and could wield magic.

I didn't agree.

There was more to Alice than met the eye—that was a fact, or she wouldn't have been able to open the circle like she did. But a witch? I'd seen the witches forced to do the

Syndicate's dirty work, and she was nothing like any of them. Nor did the cloying stench of magic I was used to smelling every time I was around a witch cling to her skin.

Tilting my head to the side, I examined her closely like I'd been doing the last few days. Ever since we managed to escape the attack from the Syndicate with our lives by the skin of our teeth. It wasn't easy running with Johnathan flung over my shoulder like a sack of potatoes while dodging Dominic's attempts of taking him so he could carry the weight. It was as endearing as it was annoying.

We found the old vehicle Alice's father had for emergencies with ease, and after a lot of praying and rattling of the rusted contraption, we left our troubles behind. Or so I hoped, anyway, at least for a while until I could think of what to do. My heart skipped a beat every time I thought about that night and what could've happened if her late father was not as paranoid as he had been before passing away. Thanks to the poor human's distrust and fascination with alien lifeforms, the three of us were alive to this day.

I'd caught Dominic looking at Alice too, but surprisingly he was being very clinical about it. Clinical *and* suspicious, and much more than necessary. Not that I wanted him to look at her with interest or anything. Just that he was a male, and Alice was a very beautiful, albeit quirky and strange, woman. The shifter's trust issues notwithstanding, nature was bound to steer his hormones in that direction. Wouldn't it?

"Well?" Alice prompted me, a line forming between her brows while she pushed the frames perched on her nose up with her forefinger. I was grateful she pulled me away from the silly thoughts swirling through my mind.

"Vampires are made up creatures the humans love to

2

read about, Alice. We talked about this many times. My kind are called Atua, and we do not bite humans to change them into one of us. Also, blood itself is not what sustains us; it's the lifeforce in it we need."

The sign might've been unnecessary, especially because she didn't really frustrate me with her insistence of my being a creature from fairytales. The Grimm kind of tales, if I remembered correctly, but a fictional one, nonetheless. I was just feeling the effect the daylight had on my kind down to my marrow as the early dawn slowly crept up the sky. Exhaustion tugged on my senses, and my mind was processing the exchange sluggishly. I should've slept, but I enjoyed talking to Alice too much to miss any opportunity to do so. In all the time I've known her, our exchanges were short and to the point. I did all I could to keep her away from the Syndicate's notice.

"You drink blood." The twist of her features told me she was not convinced that I was giving her the truth. "Maybe Atsua ..."

"Atua," I corrected earning myself a flat, pointed look.

"Maybe Atua," she pronounced it slowly, which I assumed was for the benefit of my addled brain. "Means vampires only in your own language. You just don't know it?" It came out as a question, and I answered only because I had a feeling she needed to talk and not think of the situation we found ourselves in. Or the dead shifter we left behind.

"What I believe is I know what I am since I've been the same being for centuries." I just couldn't help it with her, my lips twitched at the corners.

"You're making fun of me." She huffed, jerking on the recliner and crossing her arms petulantly.

3

I laughed.

Just a short outburst of sound, good-naturedly. She was curious by nature and obsessed with everything that wasn't human, her kennel a large statement of that. I guess I fell under the same umbrella as all her cats and dogs because she was hell bent on figuring me out. *Or she can sense if any creature is broken and she wants to heal it*, a voice in my head pointed out, and I swallowed thickly, all the humor draining from me.

"Should I lie to you and say you are right only to spare your fragile feelings?" My left eyebrow pulled on my fore-head when it raised. "I will give you nothing but the truth where I can, because the only reason I would not do that is if it will put your life in danger more than it already is. I will never lie to you Alice, but I can't share everything for your safety's sake."

With lips pressed in a firm line, she just stared at me.

"You know this is the truth, do you not?"

"I don't know, Brooklyn." Flinging both her arms in the air in frustration, she groaned and buried her face in her hands. "Vampire makes sense to me. That's the reference my brain can process. You drink blood, for goodness sake. Full on chomping with those pincers like a fiend, you know what I mean?"

Words muffed through her hands, she giggled uneasily. Very slowly, her fingers spread so she could peer at me through them.

"Say something, because I feel like I'm offending you but you're being too nice to the little human with a monkey brain." Uncovering her pretty face, she gave me a sheepish look. "Please?" For a second, the smudges she left on her glasses took my attention, but I shook it off. I had to catch a couple of hours sleep or I'd pass out on the chair I was occupying.

"Okay."

"That's it? Just okay?"

"If it will be easier for you to accept the fact I'm not human while giving me your trust so I can protect you, I will be a vampire." A soft breeze gently grazed the skin on my neck exposed from the ponytail, coming from behind me. I fought the need to smile. "I'll even be a shifter if it'll help you process better. Just don't ask me to purr while you scratch my belly, and I'm not good at hacking out hairballs."

The owlish look on her face was priceless.

"You're getting better at noticing my presence." Dominic's rasp as he entered the small room sent a shiver down my back. "I was being stealthier than usual."

I didn't point out that after our conversation, when he shared why he wanted revenge, I'd been too aware of him for my own well-being. His scent reached me just a moment before I felt the shift in the air. My every nerve ending was honed to him like a tuning fork. No matter what I was doing, including running for my life with Johnathan slung over my shoulder, I knew every move he made, every twitch of a muscle. If I was smart, I would've been worried. Considering I was on the run from the deadliest masters of the underground, how smart I actually was might be debatable.

" I can learn a few new tricks ..." I kept my tone conversational as he stepped out from behind me, aiming for the third and only other armchair in the room. "... occasionally."

"Mhhh ..." The rumble came from deep in his chest as

he lowered himself, a heavy sigh falling from his lips. Goose-bumps appeared on my arms when I took in his muscular form and tousled hair.

"Well?" Alice was frowning at the shifter. "Are you going to tell us, or do I have to pull the words out of your mouth every time. What is wrong with you guys? We all know what's happening, so telling without waiting to be asked is what normal people do."

"For one, we are not people, human." There was no fire in Dominic's tone, but it made Alice cringe anyway. My hand clenched in a fist seeing her reaction, but I didn't think punching the shifter would solve any problems. We were all tired and snappy. "As for the scum, he hasn't woken yet."

The intensity of his green eyes when they landed on my face took my breath away. It was almost a physical sensation, as if he reached inside me to grab hold of my lungs and squeezed. His animal stared at me through his irises with a primal, predatory glint, as if he was challenging me. Daring me to even twitch so I would become his hunted prey. Something that should've fired up my instincts and made me lunge for his throat, but it didn't.

"That is unusual. It was only a broken neck." Realizing my hand had moved to reach for my pendant, I lowered it immediately.

It didn't go unnoticed by Dominic, but he was kind enough not to say anything about it. Veronica's voice floated through my mind *"You're slipping. Pay attention."* And with it, a fist squeezed around my lungs and cut off all the oxygen from passing my airways.

"Which would make any normal person meet his maker," Alice muttered under her breath, but I ignored the comment. My human friend, although very open-minded, still struggled with the concept of creatures like us existing outside of fiction books.

"I wouldn't insult you by asking if you are sure, and he is not pretending," I told Dominic as an offhanded compliment, which earned me a twitch of his mouth.

"Is there a way he could prolong the healing knowing there is an interrogation waiting for him the moment he is awake?" Although his tone was even, I couldn't help noticing the dark smudges under the shifter's eyes. He's been at it day and night ever since we got here.

Me? I've tried my best to pretend we didn't have an unconscious male tied to a chair in the basement. My past and my present threatened to crash on top of my head, and I was determined to ignore it until the bitter end.

"We can control our healing, to a point." Searching his gaze, I debated how much to tell him. Airing out our weaknesses would do me no good if he decided he didn't want to play nice anymore and start his revenge on the Syndicate with me. Nothing in his behavior so far said he would do that, but better be safe than sorry. "I think we should all get some rest first. I'm too tired to deal with the likes of him, and I might end up killing the one person that could give us the answers we need. I will check on Johnathan after I wake up. Now we sleep. Including you, Alice."

"I don't feel like sleeping. I'm not tired," was her immediate rebuke a second before a big yawn made her jaw crack. Like a young child, my friend was afraid she would miss something if she didn't keep an eye on us at all times.

"You were saying, human?" Dominic glowered at her.

"I'm not a toddler, and you are not my father, cat," Alice snarked, folding her arms across her chest stubbornly. If I wasn't forcing my eyes to stay open, I would've laughed at the expression on Dominic's face. "You can't send me to bed."

"But I can." I should've thought better of it before kneeling in front of her chair and locking her in my gaze. "Sleep." Alice slumped in the recliner, her features softening immediately as her breathing evened out.

I froze, my heart lodging in my throat.

Swallowing thickly, my head turned slowly to the side, and my gaze locked on Dominic's. The shifter was as tense as I was, while his green irises burned all the way to my core. I could see the emotions playing on his features when he realized I had the power of mind control. It all played out from shock, to rage and finally settled on suspicion. What little headway I made with him to build trust between us shattered like a house made of glass under a giant's foot. Tears prickled the back of my eyes as I called myself stupid many times in my head. Knowing that Alice would force herself to stay awake, I didn't think about what I was doing. All I wanted was for my human friend to get some rest, and by idiotically acting on impulse, I showed Dominic something that not even Veronica knew.

Panic clawed my insides.

A muscle ticked in Dominic's jaw before his lips parted. I braced myself for whatever accusations he was about to throw at me, but he thought better of it. Clamping his lips shut in a firm line, he shook his head and uncurled from the armchair, fists clenched at his sides. Since I was still kneeling in front of Alice, I had to crane my neck to keep eye contact with him. A flutter in my chest told me I expected him to attack. My entire body was poised in preparation for it. He stood looming over me for a few long moments before turning on his heel and stomping out of the small room.

"Take the human to her bed. She will be useless if we

need to run tomorrow if she sleeps in that chair." He snarled over his shoulder before closing the door.

I released the breath I was holding after he was gone. Just because he walked away didn't mean he wouldn't attack. Clenching my jaw, I lifted Alice in my arms. There would be no sleeping for me this day.

At last, I'd be alert if we were discovered during the daytime. There was a silver lining in everything.

# Chapter Two

"What the fuck did you do to me, Brooklyn?"

Something hard jabbed me in the forehead as my brain jerked to alertness a second later. On instinct, my hand shot out, and I wrapped my fingers around a soft neck. When Alice's face came into focus, I recoiled, jumping away from her as if burned. My heart galloped in my chest when I realized what I had done and that I almost killed my friend. Alice, on the other hand, didn't look disturbed at all by what just happened. Her delicate features twisted in a snarl, and she bared her teeth at me.

"What did you do?" She got agitated when her glasses slid down her nose, so she shoved them up none too gently.

Darting my gaze around, I scanned the room—Alice's room, where I took her in the morning so she could sleep in her bed. I kept vigil perched on a chair close to the end of her bed, but I must've drifted off at some point during the day. The fact I was the subject of the human's anger said the shifter didn't attack while I was at my weakest. I wasn't sure if I was happy or mad about that.

"Stayed by your side to keep you safe?" Arching an eyebrow, I watched in fascination as everything she was thinking was clearly displayed on her face.

Dust still coated the furniture in the small bedroom, sticking to the surface of the light-colored wood despite the sheets covering it when we arrived. The chips in the metal frame of the bed made me assume it was from use, until Alice explained the place was furnished with stuff humans left on the side of the road when they didn't need it anymore. Neither her parents or Alice had stayed in the house longer than a day or two when they were stocking up supplies. Knowing that didn't prevent the ping in my chest when I looked at everything. It spoke of a family. Crazy or not, her father did everything he could to assure their safety.

The only one that cared for my safety for as long as I remembered was me. And Veronica, but she paid for it with her life. The thought almost sent me to my knees.

"You did some weird vampire juju to force me to sleep." Undeterred that she had an enforcer of the Syndicate, a deadly creature poised to attack, in her room, she stomped closer and jabbed me with her forefinger in the middle of my forehead. "Don't pretend like you don't know what I'm talking about."

"I'm sorry." I had no idea for the life of me why I was apologizing. To a human.

"Oh," Alice seemed taken aback by it as well as she blinked at me in confusion. I couldn't help but notice she looked well rested, while a throbbing heartbeat was developing behind my eyes. "Well, I didn't expect that."

"What? That I would apologize?" Straightening, I rolled my shoulders to loosen up the kinks in my back from sitting on a plastic chair for hours. This headache was going to be a bitch. I could feel it coming.

"Yeah, usually people would try to lie so they manipulate you into thinking you are being an ass and they don't have to feel guilty about whatever they did to you." She avoided my gaze by straightening the threadbare quilt over the double bed before fluffing up the pillow. A cloud of dust puffed in her face, making her cough. "Holy shit, I'll need to scrub my face with sandpaper to clean it after drooling all over that." She threw the pillow in disgust.

"I told you I'll never lie to you." I was aware that I was having this ridiculous conversation because I was stalling. When I walked out through the door, I'd come face to face with Dominic and Johnathan, so I wanted to delay it as much as possible.

"Can Dominic do it, too?" Alice turned around so fast she toppled on top of the bed before scrambling back to her feet.

"What?" Lost in my dread, I didn't understand what she was asking.

"Can Dominic force me to sleep, too?" Her eyes were so wide it was comical. "Because he is an asshole, and he would do it every time I annoy him and wants to shut me up."

"He cannot. Alice ..." My mind spun trying to think of a way to ask her not to repeat what I could do to anyone, but she spoke over me.

"Thank God." She blew out a heavy sigh, her shoulders slumping. "I can just hear him now. You are annoying, human, sleep." Deepening her voice, she mimicked the shifter perfectly.

I cracked a smile, and she giggled.

"Don't let him hear you," I muttered a moment too late.

"Since both of you are awake, we have things to do." Dominic beat me to it, calling out from somewhere in the house. Damn shifter hearing. Panic tried to choke me, but I forced it down. Whatever happened, I'd deal with it as it came.

Alice blanched, her mouth hanging open. "He will rip my tongue out." She breathed, and by that she made me laugh despite the dread churning in my stomach.

"He will not hurt you, Alice. The shifter might be grumpy as hell, but he is not a ruthless killer." I sure hoped my words were true, for both our sakes.

"Says Wonder Woman, who can break him in half. If you forgot, I'm the human." She hissed and jabbed a thumb at the center of her chest. "I can't hold an entire roof on my shoulders to save us all. He can snap me like a twig."

"I will snap you in half if you don't come out of there," the shifter in question hollered from behind the closed door.

Alice gulped.

"Come on." Ushering her in front of me, I guided her through the narrow hall toward the kitchen where I could hear Dominic moving around. "The longer he waits, the more he'll prickle like a porcupine."

"Are you trying to get me killed?" Alice dug her heels in, gawking at me over her shoulder. "Because let me tell you one thing about us humans. If our neck breaks, we don't heal, Brooklyn. We die. Like caput, deader than dead. A corpse."

"I'm aware what dead looks like." Nudging her to move, I had to bite my lips so I didn't smile.

I wasn't sure Alice knew how refreshing she was to Dominic and me. In our world, no one spoke their mind the way she did. It was all measured words meant to manipulate, as she accused humans of doing earlier, or to make sure you didn't give yourself away and offend someone so much it would cost you your life. I couldn't decide what that said about my human friend. She was naïve, or she had no self-preservation. The third option was that she blindly trusted me with her life. That warmed the emptiness I felt in my chest after losing Veronica yet it scared me, too. Or was I too jaded and broken to be able to understand Alice? What did it say about me that I was hiding things from those I said I trusted?

"You look like shit." Alice's comment snapped me out of my head.

Dominic glared at her as he dumped an omelet on a cracked plate. Another one was steaming on a second plate across from him on the small table pushed in one corner with three chairs around it. The kitchen was small to begin with, but with the shifter's presence it looked claustrophobic. So I didn't have to pay attention to him, I focused on a tilted cabinet door that had the top hinge broken and couldn't close.

"Eat," Dominic snapped at her, moving back to the old stove where a pan was spitting oil from the heat under it.

"Sorry, I didn't mean to say that out loud," Alice murmured under her nose as she darted for the chair to do what he asked.

"You say many things you shouldn't say out loud, human." I felt sorry for the eggs he was cracking in the pan.

He crushed the shells in his fist and I had no doubt he imagined either Alice's or my skull cracking between his fingers instead. Not knowing what to do with myself I shuffled my feet a foot from the door fidgeting like an idiot. For some dumb reason the shifter made me act like a youngling unable to control my actions in front of him.

"You too, Brooklyn." The deep rumble of his voice vibrated in my chest.

"You'll need to be more specific, Dominic." Proud that I

sounded calm and collected, I folded my arms across my chest.

"Eat." It took me a second to realize he actually made food, human food, for me as well.

"Are you offering?" I sassed because, for some reason, the idea of eating human food that he made freaked me out. It wasn't like I would die if I ate it, but it did nothing for me apart from messing with my stomach.

"Why don't you come and see what happens if you get anywhere near my throat?" Dominic finally faced me, grinning from ear to ear. It wasn't a nice grin, no. It was a baring of teeth, a challenge for a fight to the death. The fact that I noticed how his shirt stretched across his shoulders and his jeans hung low on his narrow waist spoke volumes about my insanity. He didn't look like he slept either.

"I could do the wrist, too. I'm not picky," I drawled just to annoy him, and my shoulder rolled in a shrug as I took my seat at the table, staring at the omelet like it was some unknown creature that would bite me.

His low snarl made me shiver.

"You could also do the inner thigh," Alice chirped, forgetting all about being afraid of Dominic breaking her in half as she attempted to straighten her clothing that she slept in. "What? In books, vampires suck on the inner thigh, too. Well, in steamy novels, but yeah. Like, it's more intimate, or something ..." Eyes widening, she trailed off before ducking her head toward the plate, almost burying her nose in the omelet.

Great. Now all I could think was Dominic spread like an offering in front of me and my fangs buried in his thigh. My gums throbbed uncomfortably, and to cover it up, I shoveled a forkful of the eggs in my mouth. The food was still hot, so my tongue was on fire, but I managed not to spit it out. I could feel his eyes drilling holes at the side of my head.

"When you are done eating, we will go wake the scum up," the shifter grumbled, dumping eggs on his own plate.

I didn't remind him that I was one of the scum, too.

It was difficult to swallow the food through the lump in my throat.

# Chapter Three

"He's been like this since we tied him to the chair." Dominic lifted Johnathan's head by a fistful of hair.

I followed him to the basement after we ate the food in awkward silence. Alice stayed in the kitchen under the excuse of washing dishes—which there were only three plates, three forks, and three pans, so that excuse sucked—so we went to the trap door, unlatching it and disappearing inside. I didn't point out there were only three plates, three forks and a pan. I didn't want her anywhere near Johnathan. At the same time, I was thankful that the shifter decided to ignore what happened that morning, too. With everything turning upside down in my life, I could only handle one clusterfuck at a time, thank you very much.

The basement we occupied was all concrete walls with no windows, resembling a tomb. My heartrate sped up and my breaths came in short puffs, but I clenched my fists and didn't say a word. Dominic didn't need more reasons to get rid of me. Knowing my secret was bad enough. Every wall under the house was lined with roughly made wooden shelves packed to the brim with canned foods, and the bottom had twenty-five-gallon bottles of water stacked all around it. In the center of the concrete floor was a drain, and a rusted pipe stuck out in one corner with a weird looking faucet screwed on top of it. Alice told us the pipe was connected to a large tank of drinkable water, which was buried somewhere around the property. A perfect space to withstand an apocalypse if ever I saw one.

Johnathan was slumped on a chair in the middle of it with thick ropes wrapped around him from his shoulders to his ankles, and his head hung limply down to his chest. His perfectly tailored suit was ripped and dirty, and his hair was sticking out in all directions thanks to Dominic's rough handling. I didn't complain about the treatment he received. Knowing him, I'd want to kill him myself the moment he woke up and opened his mouth. I also didn't point out that we didn't secure anything to prevent him from jumping off it, but he did wrap our prisoner like a mummy to the chair regardless.

"He should be awake by now." Inching closer to where the male was held by the ropes, I reached for his neck. Before the tips of my fingers made contact with the skin, Dominic snatched my wrist in a bruising grip.

Frowning, I turned to face him, wondering if he decided to address our little problem now that we were away from my human friend. It occurred to me that he could kill me and Johnathan in the basement and tell Alice we killed each other if he wanted to use her and the house as a safe place to lay low for a while. With a sharp pain, my fangs slid from my gums, and I stiffened. Confusion clouded my mind when I realized he wasn't glaring at me with murder written all over his handsome face. His eyes were narrowed at the base of my throat where the pendant sat pressed to my skin.

"It's not glowing anymore," he murmured deep under his breath.

"What are you talking about?" I tugged on my wrist to let him know I wanted him to release his hold, but his fingers tightened.

"When you reached for him, it started glowing." The intense gaze lifted from my neck to my face, the green irises glowing like lanterns. "Your pendant."

"It's never glowed before." It was more like a choker around my neck, so there was no way for me to see it while I was wearing it. "Are you sure it wasn't a reflection of the light playing tricks on your mind?" The yellow bulb was hanging on a cord above our heads, swaying gently.

"It wasn't a reflection of the light." I became acutely aware of how close he was standing.

With every word he spoke, his breath grazed my skin, and his scent filled my nostrils. The panic I was fighting from tight spaces was replaced by the stuttering of my heart from his nearness. My skin felt like it was on fire where his thick fingers were wrapped around my wrist. Despite all that, he kept his gaze locked on mine as if staring at me would give him answers that I would deny him. Pushing down the initial reaction that would've assured one of us might die in the basement, I took a deep breath and decided to try a different approach. I would test the waters, so to speak.

"I trust you." My heart jumped to the roof of my mouth as I said the words, and a sharp pang stabbed me in the chest when he jerked like I'd slapped him. "I just can't see it right now, and I've never seen the stone glow since I've had it around my neck."

Dominic was a highly intelligent male. He knew what I was doing, and his eyes narrowed at me. I stood still, even as his free hand lifted and he wrapped his fingers around my throat. The moment of truth was happening, and every muscle in my body coiled tightly as if ready to snap. His breathing deepened, and his chest puffed high enough that it brushed against mine with each inhale.

"Every instinct I have screams at me to kill you right now, Brooklyn." I knew he felt the hard swallow as I tried to push down the lump choking me more than his hand ever could. "You are everything I've despised since that cursed day my family was taken from me. Since your kind took them from me."

"What's stopping you then?" It was surprising to hear that my voice was even like I wasn't treading the line between life and death by the skin of my teeth. If I was smart, I would have my fangs in his jugular before he blinked. "If you think my death will be enough of a sacrifice for what you have lost, take it. I will offer my life freely for your peace and would not fight you. This is no news to you, and I dislike repeating myself." And more shocking than sounding calm was the fact that I meant every word.

I wasn't a fool to believe I would live a long and happy life away from the Syndicate. Maybe the lives I had saved so far would be enough of a redemption for my sins. The Council would come for me sooner or later, even if I hid at the ends of the world, and eventually I would slip. It was inevitable. One mistake would be all it took to kiss my life goodbye. It was very freeing to accept that fact and come to terms with it.

"Your actions fuck with my animal, and it fights me every step of the way when I even think of ending your life." Judging by the expression on his face, he wasn't really happy about it. "I don't know what game you are playing, but one wrong move would be reason enough to act on what I know is the right thing to do. Give me a reason. I dare you."

"Kill me or get out of my face." My body was reacting to him, and I needed him as far away as I possibly could in this damn concrete tomb. "I'm beginning to think I'm allergic to cats, and I wouldn't want to sneeze in your face." I went as far as wrinkling my nose at him.

Clenching his jaw, it took him great effort to remove his fingers from my neck. Eyes still locked on me, he took one step back, then another, until he almost bumped into the shelving behind him. Tucking his hands under his armpits, he cocked an eyebrow at me as if asking what am I waiting for. After a moment, I turned to Johnathan, wondering why I was a glutton for punishment. If life had taught me anything, it was that every time I allowed emotions or hormones to cloud my judgment, I only opened myself to suffering. You'd think I'd eventually learn.

Disgusted at myself, I didn't reach for Johnathan slowly like the first time. My fingers pressed on his neck, searching for a pulse, but I had no time to find any. An electric current zapped from my hand, making him jerk in the chair, and the pendant around his neck flashed brightly, blinding me for a second. Dominic shouted something, but I was too busy blinking away the dark spots dancing in front of my eyes to pay attention to his words. I did find myself plastered to his chest, and a thick arm was wrapped around my waist, holding me upright. For a second, I thought whatever happened was one of the reasons Dominic needed to kill me, but since I kept breathing, I looked around in confusion. The shifter wasn't trying to end my life, much to my surprise.

Dominic was protecting me.

"What in the actual fuck is going on?" I was finally able to understand his words.

Johnathan was snarling at us, saliva dripping from his fangs and dribbling down his chin. His eyes were shining like liquid silver on his twisted face, and the rope that was wrapped around his torso was unraveling while he thrashed wildly in the restraints. The fog in my head cleared in an instant, and yanking Dominic's arm away from me, I lunged for the end of the rope that was snaking in the air. As soon as my hands took hold of it, I planted both feet on the concrete and tugged with everything in me. The strength of my pull almost toppled the chair over. It rattled on two legs before thumping harshly on the floor. Johnathan's displeasure was a tangible thing in the stale air of the basement. Dominic was already behind the male, his hand half shifted and his claws sunk an inch into Johnathan's throat.

"What have you done?" The jerk had the audacity to snarl at me.

"Took you out on a date," I chirped while struggling to calm my heartrate down. "What? You don't like it? I thought it was quite romantic."

"You stupid bitch," he screamed and jerked my way, only to gasp when Dominic's claws embedded themselves deeper in his flesh.

"Thank you?" Both males startled at my words gaping at me like I was crazy. "What? What is it with you and calling females a bitch like it's supposed to be an insult?"

"Move again, scum. I'm looking forward to bathing in your blood." Dominic recovered first, tightening his hold around the Atua's neck.

The deep snarl from the shifter gave even me a pause. He was looming over the chair with his jaw shifting and teeth as long as my forefinger lengthening from under his lips. Johnathan paled more than I'd ever seen him, but I needed answers from him, so I tightened my hold on the rope in case he did move. He was an asshole like that, and I swore he did it just to piss me off.

"Why did it take so long for you to heal?" I had to force myself to speak because Dominic was holding his control by a thread.

"Fuck you, Brooklyn," he spat the words, fury dripping from them.

I grinned at him.

"You missed your chance for fucking, Johnathan, because you were too busy kissing ass with the Council and trying to get me killed. Now it's either talking or dying. You choose." A strangled yelp came from him when the shifter shook him by the neck. Dominic's glower sharpened from my comment, if that was possible, and something stupidly fluttered in my chest from his reaction.

"They'll find you, you dumb bitch. And I'll die happy knowing what they'll do to you when it happens." A crazed laugh gurgled from his lips.

"Why did it take you that long to heal?" I yanked hard on the rope, digging it into his chest.

"I have nothing to say to you." Blood dribbled down his chin. "I told the Council they should've killed you all those years ago, but the old fools care more about power than they do their own lives." The idiot twisted in the chair so he could look up at Dominic, almost ripping his own throat out with the movement. "And if you think we didn't know that it's you who made all those attacks on the Syndicate, you are as big of an idiot as she is. The Council has great plans for you, Dominic. You'll regret the day you came out of that bitch of a mother of yours. Do you know how she screamed before she died?"

"Dominic, don't!" My shout stopped the shifter from killing the jerk, but his entire body was trembling from the restraint. "He is saying anything to make sure we kill him so he doesn't talk. Please."

"There is nothing he can say that we won't find out from another." Goosebumps popped out on my skin from his voice. It wasn't Dominic talking to me anymore. It was a creature from my worst nightmares speaking through his deformed mouth.

"He is close to the Council, Dominic." Maybe if I kept repeating his name some humanity would return. It was worth a try. "If we want to find out what they were planning, apart from killing us, Johnathan is our best bet."

"I'm not telling you anything, you stupid bitch," Johnathan sneered at the same time as Dominic spoke.

"He won't share any information willingly." The deep growl came from the center of his chest. "I'm game to torture him until he breaks." The smile he offered was chilling to the bone.

I pushed down my dread, squaring my shoulders.

"He doesn't need to be willing." Dominic jerked his gaze from Johnathan to me. The green orbs were so intense my knees buckled. "I can make him talk."

The cat was out of the bag anyway—pun intended—since that morning, and I had nothing to lose. Might as well take advantage of it. Hopefully I wouldn't perish with Johnathan in the claustrophobic basement after he tells us everything he knows.

And if I do, I'll pray that after he kills me, Dominic will be kind to Alice and protect her for as long as she needs it. I was gambling based on the shifter's honor and his word, but it was all I had.

Either way, I had no intention on fighting him if he decided to take my life.

# Chapter Four

Unease crept into Johnathan's feverish gaze when Dominic gave me a short, sharp nod. He would've been long dead if he hadn't been smart enough to pick up on clues to alert him that something was going on. Unfortunately for him, nothing could've prepared him for the sort of freak I was. His cunning was what kept him alive and in the good graces of the Council for as long as he'd been alive. That made him a jerk, not dumb.

It hurt, however, to notice the way Dominic tensed when I cleared my throat. The shifter might've been willing for me to use any means necessary to get information, but that didn't mean he liked it. If anything, he seemed on edge and ready to attack if I turned my curse on him. I didn't blame him for not trusting me. I understood more than he would ever know.

It just didn't sit well with me.

All the fragile progress we made when it came to trust was gone and we were back to life threats. Not for the first time, I wondered what I'd done wrong to have this much bad luck in life. Humans liked to complain about their fate or lousy fortune. In the best case, they only had to deal with it for eighty, ninety years. I, on the other hand, had centuries on my plate. Realizing I just stood there stuck in my own head, I offered Dominic a tight-lipped smile.

I almost jumped out of my skin when a shrill scream came from above us.

I could see in Dominic's face he was about to kill Johnathan, not trusting he would stay tied down here if we left, so I made a split-second decision. Moving with speed my kind was known for, I wrenched Johnathan's head, breaking his neck again. He went limp on the chair, but I couldn't waste time. Alice was in trouble. The most terrifying scenarios played in my head as I broke through the trapdoor and bolted through the house like a demon on steroids. Dominic's muttered curses followed in my wake as the shifter rushed to join me. My ears strained to hear my friend's heartbeat, and I veered toward the small living room.

The trapdoor for the basement was on the floor of the tiny kitchen, so I didn't have much space separating me from Alice. A foot from the entrance, I stopped dead in my tracks, every muscle tensing when my knees bent. Dominic barreled past, bumping into my shoulder and making me stumble to my right. That placed us in the perfect position to surround the Atua that had his hand wrapped around Alice's throat, her back pressed to his front while she clawed at his wrist as he grinned at me from next to the broken window. I'd never seen this male before, but his bare chest, leather pants, and the damn pendant sitting inconspicuously on the hollow of his throat told me everything I needed to know. His shorn dark hair glinted like oil in the yellow light of the lamp, and although he was grinning, there was not an ounce of humor in the harsh lines of his face.

Dominic snarled deep in his chest.

"It's me that you want." Proud that the panic didn't reflect in the tone of my voice, I did my best to straighten from my fighting stance and look resigned. "I'll come willingly, let the human go."

The Guardian of the Syndicate narrowed his glossy blue eyes at me, his look telling me he didn't believe a word coming out of my mouth. The plate-sized hand around Alice's neck tightened, as well, and she made a whimpering sound that shredded my heart. Her face looked almost blue from lack of oxygen because the idiot couldn't understand how fragile humans were. My skin prickled from the power blasting out of the shifter, who was too still for anyone's good. I felt his shift coming and was shocked he wasn't already down on all fours.

"Don't be stupid." A movement from outside the broken window told me we were probably surrounded by at least a dozen Syndicate members. "She is human and of no significance to you or the Council. Sure, you can kill her, but that will only piss me off. You see, I like my food alive. If she dies, so would you, and so would all of your buddies." Holding my gaze steady on his, I allowed one side of my lips to quirk. "Let. Her. Go."

If possible, Alice paled more when her wide eyes landed on me.

I had no idea what I looked like in that moment.

All I knew was my heart stopped beating when I saw her struggling in the Guardian's grip, and the blood in my veins was curdled into mud. Dominic was muttering something under his breath, but I couldn't hear a damn thing from the white noise in my head. I blinked twice when the Atua spoke.

"You come with us and the human lives." His voice was raw as if his vocal cords were ripped and not fully healed yet. Knowing those ancient idiots, I had no doubt that was the case.

"That's not how this shit works." Tuning into Alice's heartbeat, I wanted to rip his head off when I realized it was skipping beats, stuttering, and slowing down. "I will give you one last chance to do the right thing so all of us can walk out of this alive. Let the human go, now."

Dominic cleared his throat, and I eyed him from the corner of my eye. What in the worlds was wrong with him? When he moved after being unnaturally still from the start, all of us tensed, but he only rubbed a hand over his mouth. That's when I heard what he had been muttering the whole time.

"Talk." It was barely above whisper, and I wasn't sure the Atua didn't hear him as well.

My mind was spinning. Talk? Talk what? Isn't that what I'd been doing since we got here? Was he planning something and needed me to buy him time? Alice had no time for him to strategize, or didn't he notice? All that spun through my head in a split second before what he was asking hit me like a metal pole to the face.

"Let her go." The words were out the next second, thrumming with more power than ever before.

The Atua's fingers snapped open, his eyes glazing over.

Alice dropped on her knees, cradling her neck and hacking for all she was worth. Dominic shifted, and a black blur took the Guardian down, blood spraying from his throat in an arch that splattered on the walls. Some of it ended up all over Alice, and she choked, crawling on hands and knees toward me. I snatched her from the floor and tucked her behind my back just as I heard it.

The whisper of metal leaving its sheath.

"Oh, shit," Alice croaked, grabbing fistfuls of my shirt.

The black panther snarled, the ferocious sound lifting all the tiny hairs on my body to attention. He glided away from the dead Guardian, whose head was holding onto the rest of him by a thin flab of skin, and positioned himself between the broken window and us. Ears pinned tightly to the back of his head, he lowered, his tail lashing in jerky snaps behind him.

"Alice I need you to find a place to hide until I call you out." Reaching for the dagger I now always kept strapped to my thigh, I pulled it out and took a step forward to help Dominic.

"No," the human snapped stubbornly.

Before I could hiss back at her, she was gone from behind me, and I released a sigh. It must've been just a delayed reaction from earlier since I had no doubt she was in shock. Any normal person would be if monsters invaded their home. My steps faltered when her pattering footsteps became louder instead of fainter, but at that moment, Guardians poured through the broken window like ants after stomping on an anthill. Snarls and grunts filled the house when the panther pounced on them, instantly crushing a couple before they had a chance to crawl all the way inside. It left them draped over the windowsill like dollies, their blood from the sharp edges of the glass making dark puddles on the floor.

The front door burst into splinters, and I turned on my heal, darting to the small entrance to intercept them. Fangs bared, I slashed, punched, and kicked, bending at unnatural angles to avoid swords and daggers the Guardians aimed at my head. There were so many of them. Too many for the two of us to fight.

Panic gripped me in an iron fist.

Alice.

In all of this, she was the only innocent one, her only sin being that I singled her out and used her to do my bidding in my fruitless attempt to screw with the Syndicate. And now she would lose her life just like Veronica did because I couldn't accept my fate. For my idiotic dreams of vengeance and that life didn't have to be all about power and killing. I wanted to rid the world of monsters, and instead I'd become one, as well. Only others paid for my insubordination.

Another life would stain my soul.

Blood coated the floors and made it difficult to move gracefully, so I slashed around wildly, desperation guiding my every kick and punch. Rage cast a red haze over my vision, bathing the unfamiliar faces in a fire hue that burned my retinas. I kept swirling, tearing whoever I could reach limb from limb, using claws and fangs after the dagger slipped from my hand. Hot liquid dripped from my mouth down my chin and drenched my shirt. Every rational thought left my mind and, listening to Dominic's roars and snarls along with the Atua's screams, I simply killed.

I had to end their lives.

I had to kill them all before they took another life they wouldn't have known existed if it wasn't for me. Everything was moving on autopilot until a familiar voice penetrated my numbness. At first, I thought I'd imagined it, but it came closer and I spun around to see if I was hearing things. It cost me a broken rib and a dagger embedded to the hilt in my kidney, but I stood there gaping like a fish.

Alice was spinning around like a dervish, a large, long

knife clutched in a white-knuckled grip with both hands, and she was hacking her way toward me. Hands and fingers were dropping around her like confetti but the human didn't falter and she didn't stop. She was using the knife like a machete with a determined look pinching her face. A warrior cry full of fury and fear ripped from her throat, and she pirouetted to me, pressing her back to my back, gasping for a breath. Nothing stunned me more than her weapon of choice in a fight against killers.

My human friend was brandishing a bread knife of all things.

## Chapter Five

"Alice, what in the worlds are you doing?"

Taking hold of her upper arm, I moved her around so I was facing the broken front door. There was a low wall I had made with decapitated bodies, the heads rolled away to the sides. It forced the two Guardians who were trying to enter to crawl over their dead brethren with faces twisted in rage. Their eyes were locked on me, dismissing Alice as the lesser threat. From what I'd seen, I wasn't sure they were correct in their assessment.

"I have no idea." Alice panted, waving the bread knife left and right like a stick she'd normally use to ward off dogs.

I had no time to try and talk sense into her, so darting closer to where the Guardians were attempting to slip in so they could attack, I snatched my dagger from the puddle of blood on the floor. I stabbed the Guardian on the left through his eye, the hilt of my weapon making a dull thud when it hit his cheekbone. His scream burst my ear drums, throwing me off balance as I listed to the side, reaching for

33

the second Guardian. My arms wrapped around his shoulders in a lover's embrace, and his confusion cost him his life. Striking like a snake, my fangs ripped his Adam's apple out, spraying hot liquid over both of us.

"Brooklyn?" Alice hissed in alarm, and I spun around, blinking fast to clear out the blood dripping in my eyes.

The one Atua, whose left hand and three fingers from the right were sprinkled in the hallway thanks to Alice, was glaring at her. Shoulders hunched, he was ready to pounce, so I jumped from near the door to stand as a shield in front of her. My fast movement startled Alice, and she stabbed the breadknife at me, catching my upper arm and splitting skin and muscle as if she was using a freaking sword. My pained snarl made her jump to the side, gaping at me owlishly.

"Oh my God," Alice whimpered, lowering the damn thing. "I'm sorry. I have no idea what's wrong with it." Her knuckles were still white from how hard she was clutching the knife. "Watch out!"

Her warning saved my head since it made me instinctively step to the side. Unfortunately, I stepped to the wrong one, and the Guardian barreled into me, taking us both down. His weight pressed on top of me, mushing my nose and face in the already congealed blood on the floor. My cheekbone was screaming as he pushed his hand hard on the back of my head, pinning me with a knee wedged next to the spot I was previously stabbed at. I was coated in blood from head to toe, and not all of it was from the Guardians.

My skin was shredded in many places, so the blood loss made dark spots dance in my vision while I struggled to get him off me. The longer I kept flopping like a salmon out of the water, the more panic I felt. If he went for my neck or heart, there would be no one in this hallway to protect my human friend. When the weight was gone from me, it took me a moment to realize it. Only when a foot nudged me in the shoulder did I flinch away and roll to my knees.

"You are alive … good." Alice was looming over me, but I wasn't paying any attention to her anymore.

The breadknife she was using as a weapon had a faint yellow glow as if the sun was reflecting off the blade. The problem was, it was still the middle of the night, and the only visibility in the narrow space was the light coming from the living room and kitchen. No more Guardians were left alive around us, so I rubbed at my eyes thinking the pain and blood loss made me see things. Even after I cleaned my face as best as I could, the knife glowed until it faded and the shimmer disappeared. The screams and snarls were gone from the living room too, giving us a moment of reprieve.

"Dominic," I called just loud enough for the shifter to hear, and his low growl made my shoulders drop a notch.

He was alive.

"Give me the knife." Reaching for it, I paused with my fingers an inch from Alice's hands. She was frowning at it, her eyes glued to the blade with the glasses barely staying on her face on the tip of her nose. "Alice? I need you to give me the knife. There are no more Atua here to hurt you. Can you do that for me?"

"No." Her answer was absentminded and just a breath under her nose.

"I'm going to take it now …"

"No, Brooklyn," she huffed, finally raising her gaze to my face with a glare. I cocked an eyebrow at her annoyance. "It's not that I don't want to give you the stupid thing. I can't."

"Of course you can. I'm still able to protect you if I need to—" Tensing, I leaned back when she swung the blade and wiggled it in front of my nose.

"See?" She kept jerking the knife in front of me, her knuckles tight around it. " I can't let go of it." What little color had returned to her face drained as she locked her fear-filled stare on me. "Get it off, Brooklyn. Get it off."

"Stop moving it, Alice." I had to stop myself from reaching for it, remembering the slice she gave me with it accidentally. "Let me try and take it." My ears were trained on any sound around us in case another attack was coming, and as soon as she pointed the long knife at the floor, I jumped to my feet.

It couldn't have been easy for her to see monsters breaking into her home, the one place she expected to be safe. The shock she was experiencing must be the reason her fingers were stiff around the handle of the breadknife. Or so I thought, until the tips of my fingers grazed the knife in my attempt to take it from her and a strong electrical zap sent me flying into the doorframe and whatever was left of the front door. I landed on dead bodies, bouncing off them with a groan.

"It wasn't me," Alice squeaked when I looked at her. Her head was thrashing left and right, sending the glasses flying off her face. "I swear I didn't do it."

"I know you didn't," I rushed to assure her so she didn't go into full-on panic mode. " Just breathe, Alice. I know you'd never hurt me." Both hands at my sides lifted in a placating gesture, and I prayed that I wouldn't topple over.

"I wouldn't, Brooklyn. You must believe me." Tears leaked from the corners of her eyes, mixing with whatever blood sprayed her skin. Her dark hair had escaped her messy bun, and tendrils of it were sticking out wildly around her ashen face. "I don't know why it's glued to my hands. I used it earlier and it didn't have anything on the handle, least of all glue."

"We will remove it, I promise," I assured her, and I wished I was as confident in my words as I sounded. "Can you stay here so I can check on Dominic? Just hold the knife away from you so you don't hurt yourself. It's a lot sharper than it should be. Can you do that?"

Her head bobbed frantically, while she kept her eyes on the knife as if it'd jump and bite her if she wasn't staring at it. I took that as confirmation that she would do what I told her since it was as good as I was going to get from her at that moment. Slowly, I inched toward the entrance to the living room, keeping tabs on her from the corner of my eye. Each move made my stiff clothing rub against the cuts and bruises on my skin, and I had to clench my jaw so I didn't whimper. Atua were nearly impossible to kill, but that didn't spare us the pain when we were hurt. If anything, with our heightened senses we experienced the pain, more than double compared to our human cohabitants.

I maintained my balance with one hand gliding across the wall and moved with measured steps until I stopped between the living room and the kitchen. A quick glance in the kitchen made my sluggish heart skip a beat. A dead Atua was sprawled in the middle of it, his head a couple of feet away from his body. Glass from the broken window was sprinkled around him on the floor, reflecting the yellow light that made the shards stuck in the wide puddle of blood twinkle like stars.

I watched Alice sideways.

My human friend was the only one that was in the kitchen when the Guardians attacked. It was where she got the knife from. And apparently she decapitated an Atua.

Something not many supernaturals were able to do. I was sure he'd underestimated her since she was human, but still, it took me a moment to process what I was seeing. Turning away from it for the time being, I placed one foot over the threshold of the living room so I could have Alice still in sight.

"Dominic?"

The shifter was standing in the middle of the room, surrounded mostly by body parts. From my quick perusal, I couldn't find a whole body among the limbs littering the floor. Dried blood matted his usually shiny black fur, lumps of it clustered around his front legs and wide shoulders. His ears were still pinned to the back of his head, and he curled his upper lip to snarl at me, his tail lashing behind him. Chills slithered down my spine when his glowing emerald eyes pinned me in place.

"It's Brooklyn." Holding myself still in case any twitch would provoke him, I had to breathe through my mouth so I didn't faint. "You know me, remember? We are in this mess together, but I need you to snap out of it right now." The warning rumble coming from deep in his chest spread numbness though me.

If he attacked me, there was no way I could stop him from killing me.

I was barely standing on my feet.

"I know you are in there, Dominic, and that you're reacting on instincts right now from the adrenaline. Alice needs our help." When the panther snarled and lowered as if ready to pounce, I rushed to get the words out before he attacked. "She's not hurt, I swear. We protected her. All the Guardians are dead, but we have another problem." Those emerald orbs narrowed on me. "I can't see if you've been hurt, but I am. I'm barely standing on my feet, Dominic."

Showing weakness was out of character, but I didn't see another option to get him to shift back. "I need you to shift so we can help her before she hurts herself."

Nothing happened.

We stared at each other, the panther and I, neither of us blinking. It occurred to me that he might be hurt and couldn't shift because his animal would block him to protect him from the pain. If that was the case, neither Alice nor I were safe around him. Until he healed, he would attack with intent to kill anyone that was a threat while he was wounded. That theory went down the drain when the panther sat back on his haunches, his long, thick tail curling around him. He sat there like a house cat all hulked out, glaring at me expectantly.

I frowned at him.

"I don't have time for games, Dominic, I need you to shift back." He tensed, and if a large cat could look suspicious, the shifter sported that look.

That was when it hit me.

Dominic was waiting to see if I would force him to shift with my ability. The damn shifter was testing me while I could barely hold onto my consciousness, and I'd never been more hurt or insulted. I could no longer see Alice thanks to the dark spots that continuously spread around my vision, and the speeding of my heartbeat from Dominic's shitty behavior just added to it. The hurt, anger, and blood loss did their damage, and my knees buckled where I stood. The room spun around me, raising bile to burn the back of my throat, and I started to go down.

As if from far away, I heard Alice shout my name, but there was nothing I could do to stop what was about to happen. A million thoughts swirled through my mind, the loudest one being that I did everything I could to show both of them I wasn't like the rest of the Syndicate. I didn't deserve to be looked at with suspicion when I was always ready to give my life to save both of theirs.

Couldn't Dominic see that?

My body tilted, and as I went down, I could've sworn the panther shifted and Dominic darted toward me, but I was already too far gone to know if it was true. I hoped with everything in me that he truly did so he could help Alice. Any other scenario was unacceptable for my muddy brain.

Darkness took me before I hit the floor.

# Chapter Six

"Hold it higher. Are you mentally impaired, human?"

The deep grumble pierced the thick darkness in which I was drowning. It felt like it had been an eternity where I drifted through the pitch-black space with no direction in mind. All I remembered was the cold. A bone-deep chill that sank into the core of my being and spread through every inch of me. I thought I'd never warm up. When I became aware of my extremities, I also realized that I was shaking so bad that someone was restraining me so I didn't jump off of whatever I was laying on. It wasn't a bed because it was too hard, even for the threadbare mattress Alice used for sleeping.

"If you call me mentally impaired or human again, I swear to everything holy I'm going to stab you with this breadknife in your nose." Alice's voice was becoming clearer and stronger the longer I listened.

"You are human." Deadpanned, the same deep grumble told me it was Dominic insulting my friend again, unintentionally.

"No kidding? I would've had no idea if you didn't remind me every two minutes." Alice spoke so sweetly I started struggling to open my eyes before they attacked each other. Just the thought of that damn breadknife spiked my heartbeat.

Still, I couldn't unglue my eyelids.

A chattering sound grated on my nerves, and I hated that my arms and legs were being restricted. Unfortunately, just because my brain got online didn't mean my body did, too. The only reprieve I had in my wrestle with consciousness was the fact both of them were alive, which meant Dominic shifted back and no more Syndicate minions attacked the house. And why in all the hells were we rocking? Last time I checked we were a dozen miles outside Chicago, and there was no water anywhere near us. Why were we on a boat?

"That smart mouth of yours will not get you far with me. I'm not Brooklyn. Just do as you are told," Dominic snarled, and another sound penetrated my ears.

A low hum like a generator.

At first I thought it was the shifter growling deep in his chest, the same habit he used to intimidate everyone. Be it me or Alice, he thought sound effects were the answer to getting things his way. They weren't, but neither one of us told him that. Who were we to poop on his parade, as Alice liked to say? But it wasn't Dominic being his delightful self that was making the constant hum. I also felt vibrations that made my insides tremble.

A pained grunt and a shrill squeak made me jerk in my restraints.

Panic was overriding every other thought I had previously. Smells were registering that were foreign and familiar at the same time. Adrenaline surged through me as my trepidation grew to alarming levels. We must've been captured, and they were taking us to the Council. I redoubled my fight with coming fully awake, digging to the depths of my soul for strength. If the Syndicate took us into their territory, all three of us would wish we were dead.

"I think she's coming around." Alice spoke too close to my face, and I could feel her warm breath like a cloud of hot air over my icy skin.

*Can someone stop whatever is making the chattering noise?* I wanted to scream it, but my lips were frozen solid and no words came out.

"Brooklyn?" A shriek lodged in my throat when Dominic's thick fingers wrapped around my shoulder and shook me gently.

I had no clue what was happening, but I felt like I was about to burst into flames and turn to ash if he didn't remove his hand. A pathetic little whimper, which morphed into a moan, came from me when the contact was gone. A sharp pain in my mouth told me the chattering that was pissing me off were actually my teeth clinking together. I learned it the hard way by biting the side of my tongue and filling my mouth with blood.

"Turn her on the side." Alice sounded alarmed. "It looks like she's choking on her tongue. Hurry."

That time I did scream when Dominic's hands grabbed me, flipping me on my side like a ragdoll.

"Shit," my human friend shouted. "I didn't tell you to kill her, you jerk."

"Keep that thing away from me," Dominic snapped, his voice drenched in frustration.

Maybe the Syndicate didn't take us if they were not worried of being overheard? *Or maybe you like to tell yourself bullshit to feel better,* a stupid little voice gibed in my head.

Swallowing the mouthful of blood and locking my jaw so I didn't repeat the tongue biting again, I finally cracked my eyes open. Tensed and expecting light to burn my retinas, I sagged in relief when blessed darkness greeted me.

Then Dominic moved back, and I squeezed my eyelids shut when the glare of the light stabbed my brain.

"Too bright," I mumbled, my words barely a rasp.

There was the rustling of clothing, the thumping of feet, and through my closed eyelids, I could tell when the light was gone. Tentatively, I cracked them open for the second time, impatience gnawing at me. On a good note, the boat rocking stopped, so at least I wouldn't vomit all over myself. When I thought of it, the humming was gone too. Weird.

"Is this better?" Dominic's deep timbre popped goose-bumps over my chilled skin. His knuckles grazed my cheek, and I bit back a shout.

"Why am I cold?" I asked, or I thought I asked. I couldn't be sure that the questions weren't only in my head. "Where are we?"

"You are safe, Brooklyn." Alice leaned over me, her face coming upside down when I glanced up. "Unlike Dominic. He is lucky I haven't stabbed him by now." She snorted when the shifter muttered something unintelligible.

"Where are we? What is going on?" Now that I knew I was able to form a full sentence, I repeated my question, glancing down so I could see how I was restricted. And I blinked.

A water hose?

"Don't worry, Brooklyn, we are safe for now." Alice got animated, her head bobbing in excitement, while Dominic muttered profanities under his breath. Something about fucking insufferable humans, if I heard him correctly. "We are on a train, but it won't be for long. If I judged it correctly, we are somewhere in Wisconsin by now, so we should be jumping off soon. You see, we weren't sure that those baddies wouldn't come back, so we bolted out of there. We will just lead them away so we can double back. Guess who's idea that was?" She wiggled her eyebrows at me, grinning.

My lips twitched seeing her excited like that, but the words hit me the next second, so my simile dropped. Train? What damn train? Snaking around, I did my best to slither out of the stupid water hose they used to keep my arms and legs flush to my body. I bit the inside of my mouth so I didn't scream from the pain shooting through me with every brush of my body on the floor. This explained the rocking and the vibrations I felt, along with the constant hum.

"Why am I tied up like a lamb ready to be sacrificed?" Grumbling through clenched teeth, I freed my arms and yanked the rest of the rubber hose off my legs, all while it felt like my skin would peel off my bones. "And where is Johnathan? I hope you didn't leave him behind without anyone making sure he doesn't escape."

That last part was aimed at Dominic, and he narrowed his gaze on me. I felt like roadkill, my mouth tasted like sandpaper, and my head had a live concert with drums banging in my skull. I had no desire, nor energy for his bull-shit, so I glared back. He didn't answer but did stab the air, pointing at something in the corner resembling a pile of straw-woven sacks. On closer inspection, I noticed an outline of a body curled under them and released a sigh.

"He was going to leave him, but I think he dragged him with us just to shut me up," Alice chirped, and Dominic growled in warning. "And you were having a seizure, I think, so we just wanted to make sure you didn't hurt your-self. So we tied you up."

"Alice ..." A sharp pang stabbed me in the chest. My poor friend was still clutching the knife in both hands when I turned to look at her.

"Yeah." One of her shoulders spasmed in a shrug. "It's still stuck." She frowned at her hands. It took me a moment to realize she wasn't frowning but squinting because her glasses were missing. The guilt I escaped by being unconscious returned with a vengeance. "And you're still bleeding."

I thought the wounds were the reason for my skin being on fire until I took stock of my body. The part of the train where they hunkered down was almost empty, apart from a couple of wooden crates in the far corner and Johnathan's covered body across from me. Two sliding doors were cranked a couple of inches apart, and the light of early dawn filtered through, bringing dust motes and particles dancing around the space. My shredded shirt and pants showed unblemished skin covered in dried blood and grime, but no wounds. Until I craned my neck to look at my arms. The upper arm where Alice accidently sliced me with the unusual breadknife had the skin gaping open, and blood was oozing out of it.

I swallowed thickly. "Tell me again how this happened." Shuffling on my knees, I moved closer to where she was scraping a line on the floor with the tip of the blade.

"She claims that she doesn't remember grabbing the knife."

Dominic had his eyes trained on Alice when he spoke as if she was a threat. I didn't like the way he was looking at her one bit. Leaning his back on one wall, his knees were drawn up, and his forearms rested on them loosely. It didn't fool me for a second that he wasn't poised to attack at the smallest provocation.

"That's not true," Alice snapped, surprising me. "I said I don't remember reaching for a breadknife. Actually, I specifically remember reaching for the butcher knife on that block but ended up with this one." I flinched when she waved the blade in front of her. "I wanted to help, Brooklyn." Her eyes misted with tears. "When you told me to hide, I was going to do just that at first, but when I reached the kitchen, I saw the knives. I hate being the deadweight."

"You are not a deadweight." I waited until she lifted her eyes so she could see that I meant it. "So far, you are the one giving us shelter while we are trying to stay alive. We can talk about that later, though. Tell me what happened next." I sent a glare at Dominic when he scoffed. I understood we were all on edge, but he didn't have to be an asshole.

"I was on my way to the basement, as I said ..." She gave me a tight smile when I raised an eyebrow at her. "Not my smartest choice, I know." No kidding, with a half-tied Atua sitting on a chair there, no. Broken neck or not, Johnathan was not to be underestimated. "When I saw the knives, I darted for one, but then one of those things burst through the window and landed next to me as I reached for a weapon. I thought that was it, that he was going to gnaw on me like a Rottweiler on a juicy steak."

Alice blew a deep sigh, her shoulders slumping. "I didn't see what he had in his hand at first because I closed my eyes and braced to be attacked. When I felt his hand on mine where I already held the handle of one of the knives, my eyes snapped open, but a bright light blinded me. When my sight cleared, I saw a rock fall from his fingers, and I was holding onto this breadknife like my life depended on it."

My mind was reeling with the implications. The shifter scooted closer to us now, peering between the knife and my still bleeding arm with a deep line pinching his forehead.

His green gaze lifted to mine, and I could see the unease there. The same one that was eating a hole in my stomach.

"What?" Alice whispered. "What does that mean? Did he glue it to my hands?"

"Magic." I didn't pull my focus from Dominic. "The Guardian used a spelled stone from one of the witches the Syndicate employs. But to what end? This cut was an accident." I felt the need to point that out because Dominic was barely holding onto his control. That made his shoulders relax, if slightly.

That was when Alice hummed, and my blood turned to ice at the uncertain sound.

"Actually, I did feel the urge to stab you with it back there." Her eyes were so wide they looked too big for her face. "I didn't cut you on purpose, I swear it. But, Brooklyn …"

"I want to do it now, too." Alice gulped and a shiver slithered up my spine.

# Chapter Seven

A lot of things went through my head, but I never believed that Alice would hurt me intentionally. I trusted her, unlike Dominic, who had her pinned to the far wall with one hand wrapped around her neck. The shifter moved so fast that Alice's feet were kicking the air a foot off the floor by the time I realized what happened.

"Dominic, no." Forgetting all about the pain still drumming through me, I rushed to stand next to him and placed a hand on his forearm. He was so tense it was like holding onto a stone statue. "She will never try to hurt me, you know this. It's Alice, for fate's sake. It must be whatever spell the Guardian used that's messing with her brain."

The shifter didn't look convinced, but at least my friend's feet were firmly planted on the floor. We were all bloody, ragged, and tired messes, but the fear on Alice's face made her look so small compared to him that all my protective instincts went haywire. My fingers tightened on his arm as I struggled with indecisiveness to calm him down or punch him in the face.

"Let her go, Dominic." Acting like it was frustration forcing me to lean most of my weight on his arm instead of the fact that my head was spinning, I huffed out a breath. "I'm sure you're aware that she stands no chance against magic."

"Didn't she do magic before all this shit started?" The shifter pushed the words through clenched teeth. "How can you be sure she wasn't planted in your path if the Syndicate was aware that you were up to something?"

He had a good point, but all you needed was one look at Alice and you'd never mistake my human friend for anything but a kind, compassionate soul that got herself in trouble for only that reason. Alice had a pure soul; a blind person could see that. It was why I singled her out from all the humans I came across in the first place. It was heart-warming to think that Dominic all of a sudden decided to care for my safety that much, but I had a nagging feeling there was more to it than that. It wasn't time for useless chitchat, though, so I tugged on his arm.

"I appreciate your concern but you need to let her go." To prove my point, I moved my hand from him to Alice, taking hold of her white-knuckled grip around the handle of the knife.

"He has a point," Alice muttered, not helping the situation at all.

"Everyone needs to calm down and remove the hands from one another. Now." The whole thing was getting ridiculous. "Aren't we suppose to get off this train? It's not moving."

"We will when the humans clear out." Dominic kept his attention on Alice, and his raspy tone made me aware of how close I was standing next to him. My chest was brushing against his arm, sending a tremor through me.

"What were you saying, human? That I am right?" He nudged her neck, and her head bumped on the wooden planks behind her.

"That I did magic once. Maybe I can do it again and release this stupid knife." Alice rolled her eyes at him. "And unless you are planning on choking me to death, can you move your hand please? It's giving me the heebie-jeebies."

"Tell her to release it." It took me a second to realize Dominic was talking to me.

"What?" The shifter was watching me from the corner of his eye, confusing the crap out of me.

"Use your ..." He cleared his throat, discomfort noticeable in his tone. "Umm ... ability."

"How nice of you to call it that." My mouth twisted in a grimace, and I took a step away from him. Like it or not, he did make a good suggestion no matter how I felt about it. "Release the knife, Alice."

Dominic turned to glare at me. Scrubbing a hand over my face in frustration, I regretted it straight away. Thankfully my skin stayed on my face, although it did feel like it peeled off of it from the friction. I needed blood, a shower, a few hours of sleep, and preferably for my head to stop spinning and pounding. Not necessarily in that order. All this was the Syndicate's fault, and we were at each other's throats for it. I wanted to scream, and maybe break something. None of that changed the fact that I didn't use my curse on Alice.

"Do it, Brooklyn." Tears burned the back of my eyes at the blind trust she offered me. I didn't deserve it, but I'd take it, nonetheless.

Dominic shuffled his feet.

"Alice ..." My breath hitched when a red glow bathed their faces coming from the pendant around my neck.

"Magic made it come off your neck," Dominic reasoned. "It must be reacting to the spell they used on the human."

"Alice, release the knife." Power vibrated from my tone, accompanied by a bright red glow from the stone. I held my breath, and for the longest time nothing happened. Just when my lungs started burning, Alice gasped.

The knife clattered on the floor between us.

"Son of a bitch," Alice hissed and doubled over, cradling both hands to her chest. "Aww, hurts."

I reached to pick her up on her feet just as Dominic snatched the breadknife, glowering at it. The shifter was turning it around between his fingers while I checked on Alice. Her fingers must've cramped from holding the damn thing this long. In the middle of the squeaking and hissing when I massaged her hands, she was saying something that didn't register at first. Then her words penetrated my cotton-filled mind.

"So, I think that's the answer," she finished, watching me expectantly.

"The answer to what?"

"The wound." Her chin jutted in the direction of my still-bleeding upper arm.

When I looked down at it, dizziness shoved me sideways, and I listed to the right. Dominic dropped the knife with a loud clatter and caught me before I did a perfect swan dive for the dirty floorboards. The tight grip made me press my lips firmly so I didn't scream, but a whimper escaped anyway.

"She needs help." I'm sure he was talking to Alice, but he didn't look at her. "This is all your fault."

My mouth opened to tell him just what I thought about that comment when my gaze locked on his. The gut-wrenching fear and panic in his green irises knocked all the air from my lungs. Dominic was so strong and stoic that most of the time I forgot how the situation we found ourselves in affected him. He lost his entire family and dedicated his life to avenging their deaths. If what he told me was true, Alice and I were the first beings allowed past his walls after that tragedy. How must it feel to him to see us hunted and almost killed? All the sass evaporated from me as I held his gaze.

"I'm fine." When his jaw clenched, I amended, "I'll be fine. I'm just a little lightheaded from all the blood loss." When he eyed Alice, my head was shaking before I consciously thought of doing it. "No, Dominic. I'll continue to bleed, and it'll be pointless."

I was not feeding from Alice.

No way in hell.

"If anyone paid attention to the little human here." Shouldering her way between us, Alice craned her neck so she could stare us both down. How that was possible I had no idea, but it worked. "As I was saying, I think I know how to close her wound, but we need to get to a store."

"What are you on about?"

"Stop snapping at me. I'm a grown ass woman, not a child." I froze when she poked the shifter in the nose with her forefinger. A deep, threatening growl started in Dominic's chest. "And stop snarling and growling. I'm not scared of you. Taking care of animals is my life, if you forgot. You're just a big cat with an assholish attitude. I don't give a rat's ass if you look human most of the time."

My lips folded inward, and my nostrils flared. I tried. The fates knew I tried to hold back, but my chest was tight, and my throat burned. When it felt like my eyes were about to roll out of their sockets, I burst out laughing, slapping a hand over my mouth when the sound came off as a bark. Alice snorted before her giggles joined me. The shifter flicked his narrowed gaze from her to me a couple of times before his lips twitched.

"This is what I get for not leaving the two of you to fend for yourselves." Shaking his head, he chuckled. "Let us hear it, human, and we need to get off this shit box."

"I thought cats loved boxes," Alice chirped, then she chortled when Dominic snapped his teeth at her in a mock attack. "Okay, okay, I'll stop. I'm just giddy to have that stupid thing out of my hands."

My chest went tight for an entirely different reason. I'd had this … this feeling of belonging and comradery only for a short time, and it was ripped from me when Veronica was killed. The hole her death left filled slightly, but that only brought a new wave of guilt.

"You and me both, human," Dominic was saying, his voice pulling me from the piling dread. "What do you need from a store?"

"Salt." Alice looked smug. "Lots and lots of salt."

I flinched just thinking about salt and any contact it would have with my open wound. When Dominic grinned like a fiend, though, I squared my shoulders and stared down my nose at him. I'd be damned if I showed the large, arrogant fur-ball that I was internally freaking out already. Pushing away from them, I started for the cracked open doors, almost faceplanting when another wave of dizziness washed over me.

I ignored the kitty when he chuckled as the morning air slapped me in the face.

# Chapter Eight

"Are you okay?" Alice glanced at me, asking the same question from a minute ago.

We ended up hunkered in what looked like an abandoned warehouse next to the stopped train, which they picked as our escape vehicle. It turned out that we were in the middle of nowhere. Everywhere we looked we encountered flat fields as far as our eyes could see. There was not a house in sight, little less a store. So we spent the day stretched out between large crates waiting for night to fall. I was weakened already, and the daylight didn't help at all. Dominic carried me on one shoulder and Johnathan on the other like sacks of potatoes, much to my embarrassment.

"I'll be fine, I promise." Offering her a small smile, I squeezed her thigh in reassurance. "It'll take a lot more than blood loss to kill an Atua."

"That's not reassuring, you know," she mumbled, while Dominic tensed where he was laying across from us facing the crates. "You think some of them were still alive at the house before we left?"

"No." That I was sure of. Those I fought were all decapitated, and I had no doubt Dominic had no mercy, as well. That was when I remembered the one on the kitchen floor. "What happened after the breadknife was spelled to your hands, Alice? With the Atua," I clarified when she gave me a confused look.

"I panicked." She took a deep breath and held it before blowing it out through pursed lips. "I thought he was going to kill me, so I closed my eyes and swung the knife at his head. I swear that I didn't feel any resistance, so I thought I missed him. When I felt warm liquid spray all over me, I had to look, and by then he was on the floor with his head barely holding onto his body. I didn't mean to do it."

"I know you didn't."

"Then I heard you fighting in the hall, so I didn't care anymore." She was staring at her hands, which were folded in her lap like they were a foreign object. "I thought we were all going to die, you know." My heart broke when a tear trickled down her face. "I'm not an Amazon warrior like you, but I wanted to help you both. So I just screamed and kept swinging the knife around. It was passing through everything like through butter. How is that possible?"

"Magic," Dominic and I answered at the same time.

"I'll scout to see if any humans are still around." The shifter rolled to his feet. We saw a couple of them, probably the train driver and whoever was recording the arrival of it on the stop. "If they are gone, might as well use this place to continue our interrogations. I have no need to carry the fucker around anymore." Before we could say anything, he disappeared between the crates.

"He was really worried about you, you know," Alice murmured, while I stared unseeing at the spot where Dominic disappeared.

"Hmm?"

"Dominic." She leaned closer and lowered her tone. "When you started going down, I didn't have time to do anything apart from scream your name, but Dominic was next to you before you were halfway down. He caught you, and I've never seen an expression like that on anyone before."

My head turned slowly so I could look at her face. Her eyes were swimming with unshed tears, and the lungs shriveled in my chest. I wasn't breathing, wishing for her to continue talking and to keep her words to herself at the same time. Nothing good would come of it, and I knew it. I had no right to know what Dominic felt or why. We were enemies stuck together due to circumstance, and he proved time and time again that he would never trust me. I should tell Alice I didn't want to know.

I stayed quiet.

"It was the same look my father had when my mother died." Alice swallowed thickly. "I don't think even he looked that terrified and devastated, to be honest. It took me a good hour of talking non-stop for him to release you. He was clutching you to his chest like someone was going to steal you from him."

"Alice stop …"

"No, you listen here, Brooklyn." Her head swiveled as she craned her neck to see if the shifter was coming back. "I haven't known him for long, but I already know he is a prideful jerk. And you are as stubborn as a mule." My mouth opened to argue that fact, but she waved a hand in my face. "Don't bother denying it. I had to force our friendship on you, remember? You were like a robot the first few months, talking in short sentences and thinking if you threatened me I'd do what you asked."

My mouth snapped shut remembering the exact thing she was describing. Back then, I didn't want to get to know her as a living being. I needed someone to do the things I couldn't without being discovered, so I treated her like a means to an end. Shame crawled up my neck, heating my face.

"I'm not telling you this to make you feel guilty." My human friend was too observant for his own good. "What I'm trying to say is, you two are made for each other if both of you get your heads out of your asses and stop over-thinking shit. I know those Atutatua are evil; it doesn't take a genius to see that. But you are not them, and Dominic can talk smack and growl till kingdom come, but he knows it too. I'm just saying, don't let them stand between you."

"Atua," I corrected her absentmindedly, her words swirling through my head.

"That's what got your attention from everything I said?" She glared at me mockingly.

"I'm not sure he would ever lower the walls he built around himself enough for anyone to even take a peek at the real Dominic." Her eyes narrowed further. "He is too broken, Alice."

"And you are not?" She snorted ungracefully. "Those are all excuses, trust me. We are all broken. And you know what? That's okay, as long as that's not an excuse to stop living."

"Who knew you were so wise?" I chuckled, nudging her shoulder with mine, but I had to admit, if only to myself, that she had a very valid point.

"It's all wisdom gathered from fortune cookies." Giggling, she gave me a bump in return. "I'm starting to get a headache without the glasses." Pressing the heal of her palms to her eyes, she rubbed them.

I was on my feet placing myself between her and the scraping sound of a shoe coming from further in the warehouse. My balance was off, so I kept a hand pressed on the crates, but if anyone tried to hurt Alice I had no doubt I'd rip them to shreds. I had enough energy left to kill a handful of Atua left in me.

"It's me." Dominic's voice proceeded him.

His gaze rolled over me from head to toe when he stepped into our little hiding place, checking if I'd keel over probably. Everything Alice said was swooshing in my head, and I wished that she'd kept it to herself. I didn't want to look at the shifter with different eyes. To think he genuinely cared, not because he was simply stuck with me but because he saw something in me that told him I wasn't like the rest of the Syndicate. Because deep down, no matter how much I wanted to exterminate them all, I was exactly like the rest of my kind. A ruthless killer.

"The humans are gone, and we still have a couple of hours to waste until the train goes back." His attention was on Johnathan, who was dumped like a trash bag in one corner, his limbs twisted awkwardly. "We should wake him up."

That was a subject I was more than happy discussing. Anything to take my mind away from feelings and other ridiculous daydreaming. So I pushed off the crate and stumbled over to the Atua. His shoulders were already in my hands when I paused to look at Dominic. There was no way around it.

"I won't be able to restrain him right now." It chipped on my pride, but if I lied it could cost us one or all of our lives. Johnathan had proven many times that the only thing he cared about was himself.

"I know, that's why I brought this." My gaze dropped to

his hand, and my eyebrows crawled up to my hairline. I fully missed the three-fingers thick metal chain wrapped around his hand and forearm.

That was what happened when you start thinking about feelings.

You missed important stuff.

"What can I do?" Alice scrambled to her feet as I gave the shifter a sharp nod.

"Step between the crates, Alice. Best if he doesn't see you when he wakes because I know him. He will use you to provoke us into killing him."

I could see she wanted to argue, but she only grumbled something and ducked between two rows of the stacked-up crates. I prayed she'd stay there, but I was prepared for anything knowing my human friend. Every situation was unpredictable with her around. Dominic didn't waste any time wrapping the metal chain around Jonathan until the Atua resembled a mummy again. It was still strange that he wouldn't heal on his own, but I pushed that aside for now. As long as I could bring him back, I didn't care why he stayed down in the meantime.

When the shifter pulled on the chain to assure himself he had a good hold on it, I took a deep breath. To focus, not because the t-shirt Dominic was wearing was stretched thin across his wide chest outlining every muscle of his washboard abs like it was painted on him. Or because of his dark hair that was mussed like he'd been running his fingers through it. It wasn't because of any of it.

That was what I told myself, at least.

I almost lost my arm when the pendant glowed as soon as I made skin contact with Johnathan, and he snapped his jaws at me like a feral shark. Jerking back, I frowned at the reaction, especially when his anger turned into confusion as he looked around the space. The raw reaction betrayed his panic before he managed to school his features, and he turned a murderous glare my way, fully ignoring Dominic as if the shifter wasn't present.

"Ready to talk?" Keeping my face relaxed, I watched him evenly.

"I have nothing to say." It was said almost offhandedly because his gaze was locked on my bleeding arm, confusion twisting his face. "What game are you playing, Brooklyn?"

Dominic gave me a barely-there nod from the side.

"I have a few questions, and you will answer then truthfully." Johnathan's eyes widened comically when I used my power on him. For the first time, fear crept up in his irises. With it came incredulity mixed with disgust, but I plowed on. "Did you know that the pendants can be removed?"

His jaw clenched so tight I heard his molars crack and grind. Capillaries burst in the whites of his eyes while he fought the compulsion to answer me. Face reddening, the Atua struggled in the metal chain, and when blood trickled from the corner of his mouth, I threw myself at him, prying his jaw open. Good timing too, or he would've bitten his own tongue off. My body flinched when Dominic punched him on the side of the head.

"Go ahead, bite it off you stupid fuck," the shifter snarled in Johnathan's face. "I'll make sure you write down every single word you know like a fucking confession. Or are you planning to bite your hands off, too?"

The Atua spat a glob of blood in his face, but Dominic only grinned like some psycho. I knew if I left them to it they'd just do the same thing until one of them died. Most probably Johnathan. But he had the information I needed, so I grabbed his shoulders to turn him my way.

"Answer my question." This time I caught him by surprise since he was too busy glaring at the shifter.

"Yes, they were always able to come off." His mouth audibly snapped shut.

"Why weren't we able to take them off?" I had his full attention.

"They are spelled with magic." A muscle was jumping on one side of his face.

"Is my father dead?"

"Yes," the asshole gloated in my face.

"Is my mother dead?" I had no idea why I asked. She'd been dead since I was born.

"No." I jerked back like I'd been electrocuted, and Johnathan's eyes almost popped out of his skull. All the blood drained from his face.

"My mother is alive?" The question passed through numb lips. "Answer me," I screamed in his face when it took too long.

"Yes." The defeated sound reminded me of a dead male walking, but I didn't care. Too many things were whirling through my mind.

Dominic was unnaturally still.

"How did my father die?"

"The Council killed him."

"Is she underground in the cages?" White noise was humming in my ears and getting louder with each gasped breath.

"No." There was no longer any infliction in Johnathan's tone.

"Where is she?"

"I don't know, only the Council knows."

"Who is she?" But I received only a shake of his head.

So I punched him. Again and again until Dominic

pulled me off, wrestling with me and the chain he was holding. Not that he needed to keep Johnathan tied. The Atua
was slumped, no longer struggling to free himself. In the
meantime, my ribcage hurt from the wild hammering of my
heart. That's when Dominic asked a question and received
an answer without any compulsion help.

"What is she?" The shifter growled the words.

"Freak." That time, Johnathan spat the word, glowering
at me.

"Not Brooklyn. Her mother, what is she?" Dominic
kicked the Atua when he didn't speak straight away.

Johnathan locked his empty eyes on mine, and I
could've sworn I wasn't breathing. When a small hand
wrapped around my shoulder, I realized that Alice joined us
too, and I didn't even hear her step out from between the
crates. My heart skipped a beat, but I had no need to worry.
The Atua didn't pay her any attention at all, although I
could feel her legs press on my back where I kneeled in front
of Johnathan.

"A witch."

If Alice was not holding me upright, I would've dropped
like a rock from the shock. As things were, I plopped on my
ass, all the air whooshing out of my lungs. In the distance, I
heard Dominic cursing up a storm, but I couldn't look away
from Johnathan's face.

Witch.

My mother was a witch.

And she was alive.

That little nugget kept going through my head.

# Chapter Nine

"It's impossible," I mumbled through numb lips. My skin was tingling like ants were dancing over it. "If what he says is true, I would've known. I'd know if I had magic in my blood."

Dominic cocked an eyebrow at me. He had no right to look so tempting when I was having an existential crisis. Johnathan lied, I decided. It was the only logical explanation. I didn't compel him to tell the truth. That was it.

"And how do you explain what happened when Alice was performing the ritual?" More disturbing than the reminder of the stupid ritual was the fact that Dominic called Alice by her name instead of the human. Her gasp confirmed that my friend was witnessing the miracle along with me.

"Alice must have some magic in her bloodline." My chin jutted out stubbornly.

All of a sudden the idea of Alice being a witch sounded very plausible to me. Never mind the fact one day before it, I did everything I could to convince her otherwise. The amusement dancing in Dominic's eyes called me out on my bullshit and rubbed me all sorts of wrong. I was still breathing like a bull that just finished a rodeo run, and the humming sound between my ears didn't diminish. If anything, it was getting louder. Everything they were saying sounded like it was reaching me underwater.

Aware I was focused on what my mother was instead of her being alive because I could process it easier, I gnawed on my lower lip until a coppery taste filled my mouth. Dominic checked that Johnathan was well restrained before lowering on his haunches in front of me, and he tugged my lip from my teeth with his thumb. His hand stayed on my face, cupping my cheek, and I froze like a deer in headlights.

"Look at me," he muttered under his breath, but I stubbornly stared at his chin. What? It was a very nice chin. "Look at me, Brooklyn."

I snarled when Alice elbowed me in my kidney, my gaze snapping to Dominic's face. Instead of the pity I expected, there was only something I refused to name. My face was impassive as I stared back at him.

"I cannot imagine what is going through your head right now." Nothing. I wanted to yell nothing, but I kept my mouth shut. "If he said those same words to me, I would be destroying multiple states by now coming to find her. I don't need you to tell me that's what you want to do. I'm telling you"—His eyes bore into mine with such intensity some of the whooshing subsided—"that that's what we will do."

I physically jerked like he slapped me.

"I will make it my mission to help you find her."

Dominic's jaw was set in determination. I couldn't believe what I was hearing. The shifter spent years, if not decades, extracting revenge on the Syndicate because they killed his family. Now he was telling me he would push that aside so he could help me search for my dead mother? *She's alive, Brooklyn. Stop being stupid.* I shoved the dumb voice in the deepest recesses of my mind, puffing short breaths through my nose.

"We will find her." The strength of the conviction in that last statement almost made me faint.

"This doesn't make sense, Dominic." I finally managed to find my voice.

"What doesn't make sense?" the shifter snarled. "When it comes to the Syndicate, if he said that crocodiles were dancing on two legs for the Council giving blowjobs to everyone, I'd believe it."

A loud snort burst from Alice, and she slapped a hand over her mouth. "Sorry," she mumbled through her fingers.

"What is it?" I hated that he could read me so easily when I spent years training myself not to give anything away.

I did want to ask more questions, but all the bombs Johnathan dropped on my head already made me doubt the wisdom of going further down the rabbit hole. I needn't have worried because the ass kisser was listening to everything, and apparently, he decided to become a chatty Cathy all of a sudden.

"You made sure they would kill you, you know." The Atua sounded like he was five-thousand-years old. "Frederic has been feeding me his blood for years now. He senses everything I feel, and he already knows what transpired here."

"None of the Council can track by blood." Gaze narrowed on him, I had to tense up so I didn't gauge his traitorous eyes out.

"No Atua can compel or control the mind either." He shut me up.

"Ah, crap," Alice whimpered. "They can track us because we carried this idiot along? I knew I should've listened to Dominic and left him in the basement." All of a sudden, she brightened. "Hold one second ...."

Scrambling on her feet, she hitched her ripped-at-the-thigh pants higher and rushed behind the crates where I told her to hide before waking Johnathan up. Dominic was staring at her like she'd grown a second head, probably for the comment that she should've listened to him. I, on the other hand, was having an out of body experience, going through the motion and speech while being numb all over. Until Alice darted out from behind the stacked wooden boxes.

"I know what to do now," my human friend piped in excitedly, wielding the damn breadknife again in front of her like a sword.

All my instincts fired up and came online when I rolled away from her and jumped on my feet. Dominic did the same, both of us hunched and ready to tackle her if she turned the spelled blade our way.

"Alice put that down right now," I hissed at her, but she ignored me.

"Nuh-uh. I have to kill the jerk so no one can hurt the two of you." She lifted the knife over her head, and Dominic pounced first.

A shriek lodged in my throat when they tumbled, ending with Alice pinned on the ground like a bug. Dominic held her down with one plate-sized hand pressed firmly in the middle of her back, the knife in the other, while she flailed wildly, flopping around like a fish. Johnathan didn't bat an eye at the commotion, gazing blindly into something only he could see. It curdled what blood I had left in my veins.

"Let me go, you stupid cat." Alice gave a good attempt at a growl, but it sounded more like a mewl. "We have to kill him so they can't track us anymore."

"For all I know, they've fed me their blood too." Three sets of eyes focused on me. "I've been at the brink of death many times only to be brought back." Avoiding Dominic's face, I locked on Johnathan while struggling with phantom pains along with the present ones. "Who's blood did they give me?"

For a moment, the Atua's distant eyes cleared, and terror raked me from what I saw in them. It was like he was already dead, peering at me from the pits of hell. My knees threatened to buckle, so I locked them in place and waited. I didn't use my curse on him because he would answer or not. It made no difference anymore. As soon as night fell, we would be fighting our way out of here.

"Frederic's." The answer came nonetheless.

"Did they take my blood in the cages because of what my mother is?" I couldn't stop the words spilling from my mouth.

Johnathan lifted his gaze from where he was staring at the ground. The pity there was crippling. "You have no idea what fresh hell you unleashed, you dumb cunt. I'd start running now if I were you, not that it would do you any good."

There was nothing I hated more than the word cunt.

Rage bubbled like a volcano, exploding in my chest, and I bared my fangs in his face, forcing him to flinch. "No, you and those old fools don't know what hell you unleashed when you decided to fuck with me. You should've left me alone. You should've left Veronica alone.

Now there will be a reckoning. I'm going to level the Syndicate to the ground. Every single one of them, starting with you."

Arms wrapped around my torso like shackles, lifting me off the ground and away from Johnathan. I thrashed around, wiggling to get out of the grip, but I was too weak to overpower Dominic. The fight drained out of me when he curled his large body around me and tucked his face in my neck. Sagging in his hold, I forced the tears down, unwilling to let them spill in front of Johnathan.

"I still think we should kill him," Alice chirped and stared at me when I glanced at her over Dominic's shoulder. "What? Between the kennel collapsing over our heads and you bleeding all over the hallway at the safe house, you barely have any blood of your own left in you, little less some other vamp's."

Dominic slowly lifted his head to turn to her, too.

"Don't look at me like that. You both know I'm right." I had to wonder when my human friend became so blood-thirsty, and if the spell used on the knife had something to do with it. "Why are we letting this sniffling idiot freak us out?"

"They'll start with you, human," the Atua hissed at her, jolting me out of the shock of seeing Alice wanting to kill. Johnathan was showing emotion for the first time after I forced him to tell the truth.

My gaze narrowed on him.

"Oh yeah?" Slapping her hand on her cocked hip, she grinned at him like a crazed person. "They'll have to go through saber tooth on steroids over there first, and then through Wonder Woman to get to me, buddy. All of you vamps can kiss my ass. You don't stand a chance."

A bark of surprised laughter burst through my mouth.

It was the trigger that brought the climax of the last twenty-four hours.

Johnathan got animated, hunching forward to glare at Alice. I felt Dominic tense since I was still hugged to his chest, and he unnoticeably glided closer to place us between the Atua and our human friend.

"They will drain you very slowly, human. They'll use your blood like they'll use your body, until your mind breaks. Only then will you be granted death, but not before you beg for it on your knees." Spittle flew from his lips.

My hands clenched into fists.

"Dude, you are wrapped up like fresh sushi right now, if you didn't notice." Alice chortled in his face, but I noticed that she paled slightly. Stupidly, Dominic and I succumbed to our traumas and fell for his manipulation, but my friend was smart the way she tricked Johnathan at a great cost to her. "If the cat gives me my breadknife, I'mma file you like a fish, just so you know."

My feet hit the concrete floor when Johnathan surged, and Dominic released his hold on me. The shifter intercepted him halfway to Alice and broke his neck with a sharp twist of his arms, the muscles bunching. The moment the Atua plopped in a heap on the floor, Alice dropped on her knees, her hands shaking uncontrollably.

"It's okay, Alice." I rushed to her, throwing an arm over her shoulders, and she huddled on my chest. "It's over, and he won't hurt you. You were so brave, my friend." My other hand was rubbing her back, and I had to grind my teeth when it sent pain through me from the still-open wound.

"Brave." Alice snorted, trembling in my arms.

"I believe you are Wonder Woman. You saved our lives; Dominic and I were too lost in our own heads to see what was happening."

"I almost shit my pants, Brooklyn. You wouldn't be saying that if I stunk up the place like a skunk." But she stopped shaking, so I laughed, although it was weak.

"You did well, human." Dominic squeezed her shoulder with a crooked smile playing on his mouth.

"Thanks, cat." Alice ducked her head, her face darkening at the cheekbones. "As a payment for my bravery, you can kiss Wonder Woman once, since you deprived me of the pleasure of seeing it back at the kennel."

My brain was still trying to catch up with what she was saying when Dominic plucked me from the floor and his soft lips crashed into mine. I developed a glitch from some wires crossing in my mind because, next thing I knew, I was kissing him back. He tasted wild, almost feral, and it formed feathers to tickle the back of my throat. A strong need clawed inside me while he devoured my mouth in a life-altering way. I was well aware that something shifted with this, but I was too far gone to care. My fingers were clutching his shoulders in a bruising grip, even when he finally pulled away for air.

He'd never looked more sinful than that moment with his lips swollen and glossy from the kiss and his hair wild around his head. I assumed I didn't look any better with my mouth tingling and his taste still on my tongue. My heart was pattering for a different reason, and to escape Dominic's intent stare, I glanced at Alice.

She had a knowing smile ghosting over her face as she watched us unblinking.

Maybe she was indeed a witch. Because what she did sure looked like sorcery to me.

## Chapter Ten

No one came after us at the warehouse, or on the train while we sat in awkward silence all the way back to Chicago. Dominic wouldn't look away from me, and I pretended I didn't notice. He positioned himself on the opposite side of the wagon we slipped into just to the right of where I sat with my knees hugged to my chest. At the same time, Alice had the widest smile plastered on her face, and she pointedly stared at both of us. Johnathan was the lucky one with a broken neck and no need to feel tortured. For the time being, anyway.

I was so angry that I fell for his bullshit that I couldn't wait for the ass kisser to wake up. When he opened his eyes again, I'd personally rip his tongue out and serve it to him on a silver platter. Dominic made a great point. The Atua didn't need the ability to speak. He had two hands, so he could write.

Stewing in my own anger, my body rocked gently from the rocking of the train. The vibrations coming from the floor were soothing to a point as they spread from my ass all the way up my spine. With effort, I suppressed the urge to touch my lips, which were still tingling. I hadn't been kissed for decades. Ever since Johnathan decided to betray me. It all felt new, exciting, and scary as hell.

*What were you thinking, Brooklyn? You don't have time to pretend to be a lovesick fool. The Council is coming to kill your friend, and for your head. And your mother is alive somewhere.* I pinched my thigh really hard to stop the onslaught of thoughts.

"Am I the only one excited about the kiss you guys?" Alice couldn't contain her delight anymore. She was practically bouncing on her ass all over the floor. "No? Anyone? Tough crowd," she muttered to herself and shook her head.

Eyes closed, I leaned my head back on a sigh. The shifters gaze was burning a hole on the side of my face, so I cracked my eyelids open and peered at him through my lashes. Subconsciously, my fist rubbed at the center of my chest when tingles erupted at my center from the hunger burning in his green eyes. I couldn't remember anyone ever looking at me like that.

Goosebumps covered me from head to toe.

Dominic's nostrils flared.

"Is it just me or is it really hot in here?" Alice piped in, nudging me. I lowered my eyelids again, but not before I saw the curl of his lips at my friend's antics. It wouldn't be the Syndicate, I realized at that moment as I was drifting off in an uneasy slumber.

Alice would be the death of me.

I was sure of it.

*Shouts and snarls were louder than anything else as I shook my head to clear it. Scrambling around, I tried to stand up, but my heel got caught in the silk of my dress. I tipped to the side as I realized the damn string pretending to be my underwear was cutting between my ass cheeks, which pissed me off, too. My ribs and shoulder protested from the impact as I flailed around like a fish out of water.*

*"This is why I don't wear fucking dresses," I hissed angrily at the stupid dress when a hand wrapped around my arm and hauled me up.*

*"We have a problem." Veronica panted next to me, her nails digging into the skin of my upper arm. Internally, I was stunned to see her alive in front of me, but dream me kept going no matter how much I wanted to stop her.*

*"No shit. What gave it away?" Jerking my arm out of her grip, I tried to assess the situation.*

*"Don't be an ass, Bee. We have a shitstorm happening."*

*Everyone was running out of the hall, pulling daggers and other weapons that glinted in the light of the swinging chandeliers. Naked, barely-alive humans huddled in groups in the corners trying to make themselves look as small as possible. An explosion shook the foundations of the mansion and pitched me sideways into Veronica. We both stumbled while reaching blindly for any sort of support.*

*"What the fuck is going on?" I expected many things tonight, but this was not one of them.*

*"Someone attacked the mansion." The awe in her voice was reflected on my face.*

*"Who in their right mind would attack the Syndicate at home?"*

*"I know, right?" Her nervous laugh was contagious, so I joined her. "Listen ..." When she paused for too long, I turned to give her a quick glance. "Do you think maybe it has something to do with your jobs lately, the ones that were done but not really done?" Chewing on her lower lip, she watched me with a sheepish look. My stomach dropped. "I knew what you were doing. That's why I was hell bent on coming with you. In case we need to do a coverup or something."*

*"Veronica, I ..." Lost for what to say, all I could do was sigh and scrub a hand over my face like that would make everything better. I realized that everything after that moment happened because of me. Because of my selfishness and keeping secrets.*

"I don't need an explanation, Bee. I just want you to know I'm proud of you." Tears shimmered in her eyes. "Do you think that may have something to do with this?"

"No way." All those shifters were safely in the reservations. Hopefully they'd stay there for a very long time, too. "I have no idea what this is, but I'm about to find out."

"Where the hell do you think you are going?" She grabbed for me, clawing at my arms to stop me from leaving our safe place near the wall. The two of us were as pathetic as the humans.

"If someone is attacking the Syndicate"—Glancing around to make sure no one was listening, I leaned closer to her—"I'm going to help them."

The world around me shifted, throwing me into a different scene. I fought with everything in me to stay where I was. In a time where my friend was still alive. I failed. I failed her.

It was the second time I'd come face to face with the Council, and only someone's grip on my arm kept me standing. Seeing Veronica bloodied on her knees in the middle of the wide room cracked open my heart, and my legs almost gave out. Her bruised face shook sharply in a no, which was the only thing that stopped me from bolting to her. My gaze snapped at the three males who were watching me intently with various expressions plastered all over their faces. The leering disgust and anger I could deal with. It was the anticipation in Isaiah's eyes that sent ice shards through my center.

"Brooklyn, I am pleased to see you are unharmed." Frederic's gaze flicked to my neck where the purple and blue fingerprints of the shifter's hand had long since disappeared.

"I'm sure you are." It was out before I could stop myself. "Sire," I added lamely through my teeth.

"Come closer, child." Samir beckoned me with his hand, and Johnathan finally released the death grip he had on my arm, leaving red lines where his fingers used to be.

"You see, Brooklyn. Veronica here was not who we thought she *was." Isaiah spoke as my numb legs carried me to stand next to Samir. I curled my fingers around the seams of my pants to stop my hands from shaking. "She was in cahoots with our enemies and helping them plan an attack while we took care of her as one of our own."*

*"She is one of us," I snapped at him.*

*"Bee, don't." Veronica's cracked voice was barely above a whisper, and that sound stabbed me right in the chest. I knew I was dreaming, but seeing my friend alive opened a fresh wound that crippled me further. I wanted to run to her, and I even struggled in the dream to make my legs move, but I stood where I was, the misery strangling my throat.*

*"Is she now?" Turning his upper body to better face me, Isaiah arched an eyebrow while he eyed me like a cat would a cornered mouse.*

*"She is loyal to the Syndicate. I would place my life as an assurance." In reality, I looked away from Veronica that night, but in the dream, I kept my eyes on my friend, drinking her face in as tears rolled down my face. I knew what was going to happen, and I was dreading it. "Don't do it, don't bring attention to yourself," she mouthed, and a frown tugged on my eyebrows. Veronica never said that.*

*Was this really what happened that night? Or was my subconscious playing tricks on me in the dream? My body swayed, and the room tilted in front of my eyes when a different scene came into focus.*

*All three Council members jumped to their feet, and I flinched away from them. Frederic and Samir roared insults at Veronica, while she stood proudly facing them with a serene smile on her face. The pendant was not around her neck, the bare skin taunting me. Isaiah materialized next to her as the Guardians burst through the doors from all the shouting, daggers clutched in their hands. Veronica's gaze didn't leave mine as she mouthed, "Love you, Bee. Figure out the pendant and you will find the truth. Look at the stone."*

*Those were not the last words she said. Apart from telling me she loved me, Veronica didn't say anything else that night. Fresh agony ripped through me when the rest played out just like it happened on that cursed night. Striking like the viper he was, Isaiah sank his fangs into her neck and ripped out her throat with a firm shake of his head. Blood sprayed in a wide arch until his face was bathed in it, and Veronica's lashes fluttered before hiding her warm, brown eyes from me forever. I stood there numb and horrified, my feet glued to the floor while my mind shrieked so loud it drowned out all the other noise around me.*

"Veronica!"

My body jolted upright, my shout bouncing off the wooden planks around us. Alice was curled around me, rocking me as I sobbed into her shoulder. My human friend was smoothing her hand over my head, murmuring soothing nonsense while I held onto her as if she was the only thing stopping me from bursting into a million pieces.

# Chapter Eleven

"Stay here and guard the human while I scout the area first."

Dominic tossed Johnathan's body like a trash bag to the side and disappeared among the trees when we reached the safe house, which was no longer safe if you asked me. It was the first thing the shifter said to me after my meltdown from the nightmare on the train. While I sobbed my heart out, he sat across from us, clenching his fists as his eyes burned with fury. Whether it was aimed at my slobbering mess or the Syndicate, I wasn't sure.

Alice huddled closer to me, and I tucked her at my back in case there were goons waiting for us to return, while my head moved from side to side watching for a shift in any shadow. Lack of sleep combined with the blood loss messed me up pretty good, to the point I had no control of my body. I'd been able to block out any night terrors for years. Even the ones from the cages that used to wake me screaming and shaking like a leaf. Apparently, I couldn't stop Veronica's death from taunting me. Not that I didn't deserve it.

"You'll be okay as soon as we get inside, Brooklyn," Alice murmured, clutching my grime-covered shirt and poking her head to peek around me.

"I'm okay now." Glancing down at her, I even offered her a strained smile.

"Right." Rolling her eyes at me, she jumped when a branch snapped from somewhere to the side.

"A rabbit."

"You know how freaky it is that you actually know what kind of animal did that?" Squinting up at me to see me better without her glasses, she grinned like a loon. "I wanna be like you when I grow up."

"You are a grown woman, Alice."

"You're missing the point, Robocop."

"Why do you keep rolling your eyes?" Ignoring her snarky comment, I focused on the trees again, straining my ears so I didn't miss a sound.

"Because you are an amazing person, Brooklyn, whether you want to admit that or not. If I can say so myself, you are the type of a friend every girl dreams of when we think about times when we grow up, and also the type of woman we all hope to be." My eyebrows crawled up to my hairline when I looked back at her, and my mouth opened and closed, not knowing what to say to that. "Close your mouth, it's the truth. You are loyal and brave. You'll protect those weaker than you or the ones you care about with your last breath. But when it comes to simple things like joking, or even having five minutes of down time to simply enjoy life, you act like a robot and you don't know what to do with yourself. It seems as if that's as foreign of a concept to you as shifting into an animal or drinking blood is to me. It's quite sad, to be honest."

"In my world, you can't afford joking or to have down time. This is not a movie or one of the books you've read," I murmured under my breath, but what she said triggered that deep need I'd always felt to be part of her world. "And I'm not all that you make me out to be. Don't mistake me for something I'm not, Alice. Veronica thought I was different, that I was better than the rest of our kind. The cost for that was her life. Now it might cost you yours too, just for knowing me. I'm the same monster as those that are after us. Never forget that."

"Do you hear yourself when you talk?" Snorting, she shook her head at me like a disapproving parent. "First of all—"

"It's all clear." Dominic appeared a couple of feet in front of us, rolling his shoulders, his hair sticking out in all directions.

The way he was twisting his upper body like he was making sure his skeleton fit properly under his skin, along with the fact that I didn't hear him approaching, told me he just shifted back to his human form. His narrowed and intent gaze on me said he also heard at least half of the conversation Alice and I had in his absence, as well.

"Let's go." I was moving before I was done talking, avoiding any comments Dominic might want to add, my feet eating up the distance to the house.

"Come on, cat." Alice rushed after me, her feet rustling the leaves on the forest floor. "As I was saying. First of all"— She was skipping like a child keeping in step with me—"you are nothing like those after us. Second, believing in you and recognizing that you are an amazing person was not the reason Veronica lost her life."

"You know nothing. Do not speak of her, Alice. Let it be." I didn't mean to sound harsh, yet I did. Flinching at my tone, I didn't stop.

"Don't you dare shush me, Brooklyn." She went as far as poking me in my side. Dominic chuckled, the jerk. "Those dishrags from the Syndicate took her life because they are evil incarnate. Not because of you, or her friendship with you. Plus, they can all kiss my ass for real. You and Dominic will protect me. I'm not afraid of them."

"Unless it is me that kills you, human," Dominic growled from behind us. "You talk too much."

"Every circus needs a monkey, saber tooth." Alice snickered, oblivious to everything around her. I couldn't fathom the trust she placed in us. In monsters from her worse nightmares, of all things. "I have no problem being the monkey in our circus since the two of you are no fun at all."

"The human thinks this is an adventure of some sort," Dominic muttered low enough that only I could hear him.

I agreed with that statement but didn't voice it.

From the corner of my eye, I watched Alice. Since her glasses were gone and barely any light penetrated the tops of the trees, I had no doubt she couldn't see anything in front of her. Yet with her fingers wrapped around my upper arm, she stepped forward confidently, trusting I would lead her on the right path not to get hurt, a wide smile stretching her lips. A tight band wrapped around my lungs, restricting them from expanding enough for me to take a full breath. I couldn't let anything happen to her. I just couldn't.

When the house came into view, it gave me pause. From the outside, it didn't look like much. The faded red rooftiles were gray under the moonlight, a few of them missing here and there. One of the windows to the right was gaping open with broken shards sticking out around the frame. The front door was fully missing, and the ground in front of it had a darker color than the rest of the dirt from all the blood spilled there. No shrubs or flowers were to be seen in the empty land where it sat, resembling a long-forgotten home of humans from the past.

"I think we have enough salt in the house for what we need." As soon as we were close enough, Alice rushed inside the house, her hand outstretched in front of her. "If not, we will have to fix the car and run to the nearest store." I stopped, watching her disappear inside.

"She's still stuck on the salt." Dominic chuckled and moved past me with Johnathan slung over his shoulder. "The human is like a pest." He froze with one foot up, his head snapping to the side, and he dropped the Atua on the ground. "Get Alice," was all he snarled before he shifted.

I darted inside the house with one thought screaming in my head: get Alice. It was circling on repeat as I made a mad dash for the kitchen, finding my human friend with half her body stuck in the pantry. The light was glaring, too bright for my eyes, but I snatched her by the waist and turned toward another broken window. Alice shrieked and grabbed at me as whatever she was moving in the pantry crashed behind us. Dizziness hit me, and I stumbled, smacking my hip into the oven, which propelled me toward the sink.

"What are you doing?" Alice was shouting in my ear, making my dizziness worse. "It's not funny, Brooklyn. Put me down."

"Be quiet," I hissed at her, and she immediately shut up, her hold on me tightening.

"What's happening?" Alice whimpered, all the bravado from earlier gone.

Holding her to me with an arm wrapped around her, I

placed my other hand on the windowsill and leaped over it in a tilted arch. Not the most graceful escape but darkness covered us, and lowering her to the ground, I pressed our backs to the wall, covering her mouth with my hand. Her warm breath was puffing over my skin in short pants as she stared wide-eyed at me. Swallowing the acid burning the back of my throat, I focused on any sound that didn't belong.

Nothing.

Not even the small critters that scuttered around the trees could be heard, which told me a predator was stalking the area. I liked to believe it was Dominic, but I couldn't take any chances. From the last twenty-four hours or so, Alice was stronger than me. I couldn't fight if I had to. Holding her with whatever strength I had left, I hoped Dominic would be able to handle whatever it was. If not, we were doomed.

The ferocious cry of a large feline pebbled my skin.

Alice stopped breathing, and so did I, but no other sound could be heard in the night. That was until the shuffling of feet scraped over the dirt and a pained howl split the air.

"Brooklyn," Dominic called out, worry evident in his tone.

My heart skipped a beat, but I held Alice firmly to the wall. Did Dominic get captured and was calling to tell me to run? There was no way I was releasing Alice until I was sure she would be safe.

"Brooklyn, it's safe. I need help here," the shifter called out louder, and the whimper of a hurt animal accompanied.

Alice was gone from next to me before I could remove my hand from her mouth, running around the house like the hounds of hell were chasing her.

"Is that a hurt animal?" Her shrill tone told me she wanted to kill whoever hurt it. I darted after her just in case it wasn't as safe as Dominic made us believe. Trust issues were hard to push back.

When I rounded the house, I had to skid to a stop. My eyes bulged out, and my mouth dropped open. "Is that?"

Dominic lifted his head, his eyes locking on mine. I could tell how hard it was for him to hold the bloodied animal in his arms while Alice fussed over it, cursing up a storm. I glanced from the gray, matted fur to Dominic's face a couple of times, still unable to believe what I was seeing.

"It is," Dominic said at the same time as Alice turned to look at me over her shoulder tears running down her cheeks.

"It's the wolf, Brooklyn. He is alive." She gasped, as stunned as I was.

# Chapter Twelve

The wolf shifter was alive, although barely. His breathing was sporadic, and his heartbeat was barely there. An occasional gurgle would pass his slack jaw, the lolling tongue to the side as dry as cardboard. Dominic carried him inside with Alice, directing him like a supervisor from hell. He either jostled the wolf too much or he wasn't walking fast enough. I had no idea how he didn't snarl at her. It was the second miracle of that night. If anything, Dominic did everything in his power to do as she asked.

I stumbled after them, holding myself upright by sheer will alone. Dark spots were dancing at the corners of my eyes, and my own heart was stuttering and skipping beats in my chest. Grateful that it wasn't another attack, which I would not have survived, I was happy to tag along and let them do whatever they thought needed to be done. A fleeting thought about how the wolf found us bounced around my skull, but I was too far gone to be able to grasp it. It slipped through my fingers, leaving a distant thudding in my head.

They placed the wolf on the kitchen table, which somehow survived the fight with the Atua as I joined them. Dominic moved to the side while Alice checked the shifter for whatever she thought was important. His hind leg was twisted awkwardly, and without missing a beat, she felt through the bone before snapping it back in place. I cringed at the sound of a cracking bone.

"I have no idea how he's still alive." Dominic spoke from next to me where I was leaning on the doorframe. I didn't see him move.

"Can't you force him to shift?" I mumbled. I had no strength to speak louder, yet I cleared my throat, pretending the rasp was from disuse and not because I was ready to pass out.

"I tried, but it felt like somehow my command was blocked. When I forced it at him, it bounced back at me hard enough to make me stumble."

I could hear the apprehension in his tone. He probably thought the same thing I was thinking. The Syndicate found him, and they were using him somehow. The problem was, if he didn't shift, I had no doubt he would be gone by dawn. The shift would heal everything, and the wolf knew that, so why wasn't he? Why hadn't he done it instead of tracking us across the city and outside of it, and he did it in the terrible shape he was in? A memory teased at my senses, and I was lucid enough to examine it. The plane, the wolf shifter's fear clawing at me, his agreement to shift and wait in the luggage area until someone picked him up. Did I use my curse on him? I didn't think I did, but that could explain why he stayed with Alice and acted like a house pet. Maybe he couldn't shift.

Pushing off the frame, I stumbled toward the table. My

body tilted sideways, but Dominic was next to me in a blink of an eye, wrapping an arm around my waist. He didn't say a word, for which I was thankful as he guided me to Alice and the wolf. Leaning on the table with both hands, I blinked fast to clear my vision because I was seeing two wolves on the table and Alice had four arms. Her face was pinched in worry when she looked at me.

"Shift," I rasped, but it was barely a whisper.

"What are you doing?" Alice frowned at me. "Go sit down. I'll bring the salt and a tube. You need to eat." She said it so matter-of-factly that it cleared my haze a little. "Dominic, take her to the bedroom. She's stubborn as a mule."

"Shift." I forced some strength in my voice, ignoring her comments.

Alice screamed when the air around the wolf shimmered, and all the hairs on her arms lifted at attention. The body of the animal jerked, popped, and shifted in a matter of seconds, leaving a dark-haired male stretched out on the table. He was dirty, caked with grime and dried blood but otherwise unharmed. A sigh passed my lips seeing that it worked. In the next second, he shifted back to wolf, much to my dismay, but at least he healed. I didn't have it in me to worry about why he chose to stay in his animal form.

"Did … did that just … did he turn into …" Alice stammered, gawking from the wolf to Dominic and lastly at me. "He shifted," she told me flatly.

"He did." For whatever reason, I answered her.

"You know what? I can't deal with this right now." The shock disappeared, and she glared at me of all people. Didn't I just help her precious wolf? "Take her to the bedroom. I'm grabbing the salt," she told Dominic and stabbed a finger in the direction of the room as she rounded the table.

I didn't have it in me to argue, although I wanted to tell them that I was fine. Deep down I recognized what I was doing and how unhealthy my behavior was, but that voice was buried so deep it didn't register. Dominic swung me in his arms, and I allowed it. I told myself I *allowed* it, not that I couldn't stop him if I tried. His sinful scent filled my nose, and my head flopped on his shoulder while he carried me through the hallway.

*It was a very nice shoulder*, I thought to myself, but Dominic's chest vibrated. I realized I must've mumbled it because the damn shifter was chuckling. Too bad my arms were not obeying my commands, or I would've slapped him. When Alice came with a bag of salt like some demon from hell sent to torture me, I did wish that I slapped Dominic. My human friend didn't give me time to prepare myself. As soon as she sat on her knees on the mattress next to me, she ripped the bag of salt with her teeth, poured half of it on the open wound on my upper arm, and pressed both hands on it to grind it in all the way to my bone.

I screamed.

Agony tore through me, and it was almost like I was back in the cages held down while fangs ripped through my flesh. My own gums were throbbing, and I bared my pointed teeth in Alice's face, snarling like a feral beast. Dominic snatched my upper body, shoving me back on the bed and holding me there with one large hand pressed on my collarbone. Alice didn't even flinch. Her narrowed eyes were focused on her hands where she was grinding the cursed salt into the wound, and her lips were moving. Through the mind-numbing pain and the thundering between my ears, I did my best to pay attention to what she was saying. At first it was just a loud whoosh, whoosh, like a helicopter taking off before I could make out her words.

"Blessed salt clear the curse, heal what was wrongfully harmed." She was repeating it over and over, her voice increasing in volume the longer she spoke.

"Do you have any idea what you are doing, human?" Dominic snapped at her when I screamed bloody murder again.

"I have no fucking idea, cat," Alice hissed back. "Blessed salt, clear the curse, heal what was wrongfully harmed." She continued chanting, now shouting the words at my wound. "Unless you have a better idea, shut up and let me do this."

if I wasn't in so much pain, I would've laughed when he glared but shut his mouth. I thought my soul was ripping from the core of my being. Alice removed her hands, and I nearly sagged into the threadbare mattress. She only did that because whatever she poured into my wound had melted, and she dumped the rest of the salt on my arm before I could escape. A fresh wave of pain stabbed me with a vengeance, and I drifted between consciousness and an abyss for what felt like forever. The only tether I had to the world was Alice's voice, her chanting was more like a constant hum than words. When silence fell around us, the panic that I lost the battle jolted me fully awake. There was no pressure on my arm where my friend used to press on it.

"It worked." Alice breathed in awe.

"Well, I'll be damned." Dominic joined her, leaning over me to peer at my arm. His breath felt cold on my burning skin.

I blinked them into focus. Alice had an expression on her face like she just witnessed the heavens open and half naked angels came dancing down from it. She was gaping from my arm to her hands and back, holding them up in front of her. Dominic had a fascinated yet wary look in his green eyes when he glanced up at me. I followed his line of vision when he took my arm and twisted it this way and that to get a better look. My wound was almost gone, the skin knitting together in front of my eyes. I was still lightheaded from blood loss, but I no longer felt like if I closed my eyes I'd never open them again.

"How did you know what to say?" I croaked, my throat raw from the screaming.

"I don't know?" She sounded much younger than her age, confusion twisting her features. "It just came to me. I must've read it somewhere." Neither she nor we believed it, but no one said otherwise. "Yeah, I must've read it somewhere, that's it."

"Okay." I spoke before Dominic had a chance to say something to freak her out. The shifter closed his mouth, his brows pinched low over his eyes.

"That's it? Just okay?" Alice locked her gaze on mine, and I could tell she was thinking about saying those exact same words to me not long ago when she was convincing me that I was a vampire.

"That's it." I offered her a small smile, albeit one laced with fatigue. "Go check on the wolf." She scrambled to get off the bed and was almost at the door when I called out. "And Alice?" Gripping the door knob, she looked over her shoulder. "Thank you for helping me. You are the type of friend an Atua dreams to have when we grow up, as well."

Repeating the same words in my own way, those she told me in the woods had been the right thing to say. Alice smiled so wide my chest hurt to see it brighten her face that way. Her eyes shimmered with tears, and she filled her lungs with so much air I expected her to burst from it. With a few jerky nods, she yanked the door open and left to check on the wolf shifter.

"That was very …" Dominic sat on the edge of the bed, a strange lookin his eyes that was focused on my face. "Hmmm, how should I say it? Very unlike Atua of you." A crooked smile tilted his mouth when I gave him a huff of annoyance. "I'm afraid the human is softening you up, Brooklyn."

"You think, saber tooth?" The jab made him laugh, and I cracked a smile, too. "She's not human, Dominic." The humor evaporated from his face and mine. "Well, not fully human, I should say, because she still feels and smells like one to me."

"She feels and smells human to me, as well. But this"— He waved a hand over my now unblemished skin—"and this"—He pointed at the pendant, reminding me of the ritual Alice did to make it come off my neck—"is something only a witch can do."

"In both cases, she had my blood to aid her." If what Johnathan said was true and my mother was indeed a witch, that could be the reason. It didn't ring true, but I had no other explanation.

"I've had a witch do some talismans I needed by using blood of one of your kind. I don't think you understand what doing that does to a witch." Dominic shook his head. "It took him less than a minute to power it up, and they had to carry him out of the room unconscious. Blood magic is strong, but the price is steep." I didn't even want to know why he needed that talisman or how he knew all that.

"What are you saying? That she's not a witch?" My eyes were half mast, but I fought to stay awake. "What else could she be when she does magic?"

"She held onto the magic to heal your arm for a good ten, fifteen minutes, Brooklyn." He paused, letting the words to sink in. "And she was more energized when she finished than before she started. Alice might not be fully human, but she definitely is not a witch. Not like any witch I've ever seen, in any case."

"She is my friend, Dominic." Not liking the way he said that, I felt it prudent to cement that fact between us. "Alice can be a demon for all I care, not a hair goes missing from her head. Are we clear?"

"I mean her no harm." He snorted, glancing at me sideways. "She's annoying like a pest, but I will not hurt her. She's earned my respect without your threats."

"I didn't threaten you. I was just telling you."

"And anything coming from an Atua mouth is worse than a threat." He winked, softening the insult. Well, I couldn't take offense if it was true, so I said nothing. "Now feed."

My heart jumped to the roof of my mouth, rattling there. Dominic held my eyes as he tilted his head, offering me his neck. Stunned, I could only stare at him. His green irises began glowing softly, his animal coming to the surface and giving permission as well. I wanted nothing more than to sink my fangs in his throat, but we were in a bedroom with the door closed. And I still remembered that kiss, which brought his taste on my tongue just thinking about it. With that in mind, I reached for his wrist, bringing it to my lips without losing eye contact. I paused, waiting to see what he would do. If he got offended, he would tell me to fuck off and walk out.

I held my breath.

Dominic gave me a nod an eternity later.

As my fangs penetrated the skin on his wrist and his

blood filled my mouth, sliding down my throat, I closed my eyes and wondered. How long would I be able to resist the shifter?

How long before I fell to temptation and doomed us both to a fate worse than death?

## Chapter Thirteen

"I don't understand why the jerk doesn't shift back," Alice told me as soon as I stepped inside the kitchen. "Dude, I know you're not a dog. Just shift so I can understand what you are saying, or I swear to God I'm going to hose you down with ice-cold water." She was shaking her fist in the wolf's face. "And I'll stick a large thermometer in your ass, don't think I won't, because I do have one."

The wolf sat on his haunches, his head tilted to the side, giving her puppy eyes. Dominic was hunched over the table, covering his mouth with a hand, but the wrinkles around his eyes and the laughter dancing in their green depths gave him away. His shoulders were shaking, too.

"Maybe he still needs to heal?" I offered, hoping to help the mongrel. I couldn't understand why he wasn't shifting either, but until I was sure he wouldn't hurt her in any way, I was good with him staying a wolf. It was easier for me to judge his actions that way, plus it would be easier on Alice as well.

"I'll give him something to heal, alright, if I seriously

shove that thermometer up his ass." She huffed, planting her fists on her hips.

Dominic laughed.

Throwing his head back, a deep belly laugh bust out of him, sending butterflies in a frenzy inside my belly. I could feel his blood in me, the power in it different yet as potent as mine. Heat crept up my neck, warming my cheeks as he turned to me, his mirth-filled gaze dancing on his handsome face. The knowing look he gave me made me turn to stare at Alice. Both of them had changed just as I did when I woke up.

We no longer resembled apocalyptic refugees, thank the fates.

Alice had a black tank top and a two-sizes-too-big white shirt on, paired with dark blue jeans ripped at the knees. She rolled the sleeves up to her elbows, so they didn't dwarf her hands, no doubt. Her hair was freshly washed, falling in soft waves around her shoulders, and they must've found her glasses because they were perched on her nose with white tape holding one of the handles in place. At least the lenses were not broken. I knew it bothered her when she didn't wear them.

Dominic, on the other hand, had a grey t-shirt, a size too small, stretched over his large frame to the point of bursting at the seams. My eyebrows crawled up when I saw the black tactical pants hugging his powerful legs, but I said nothing. The place had a couple of large bins full of clothing in various sizes that were placed there just in case, or so Alice said. She never explained in case of what, and we didn't ask. The shifter's hair was also freshly washed, and I gulped when he stabbed his fingers through it, brushing it off his face. He even shaved, although the shadow from his facial hair remained dusting his jaw. The dimple on his cheek winked at me, telling me I'd been staring too long, and I jerked my gaze away. Both of them seemed better rested, which was good.

I felt much better, too.

The ping in my lower belly reminded me I felt better because of Dominic's blood. That and the magic Alice performed yet again. Skirting around the wolf planted in the middle of the kitchen, I creeped up to a chair, lowering myself on it as far away from Dominic as I could.

"They do that to cats too, you know," I murmured to the shifter and grinned when he bared his teeth at me. "Just stating facts." I lifted both my hands in a mock surrender.

"We can try to see if it works on Atua anytime you want," Dominic grumbled, not too happy about my snark.

"You checked her temperature by shoving your tongue down her throat yesterday." Alice snickered like a hyena. "Damn boy, that was really hot, if I do say so myself." She fanned her face, grinning at Dominic like a fool.

My face was on fire.

It was worse than the pain I felt when I woke up on the train.

"You can't say anything yourself and let's focus on our situation instead of stupidities." I regretted my choice of words before I was done talking, but it was too late.

The cheeky smile disappeared from Dominic's face, and I missed it the same second. Alice was also glaring at me like I'd just kicked her puppy, which made my stomach dip, and I felt sick. It was almost as if I could feel the disappointment thrumming through her like it was my own. Which was crazy because Atua didn't connect empathically to anyone unless it was a mate—that made my stomach flip flop around, too—or a mutual relationship with a donor. The Atua would need to drink blood from the person while that person took blood from the Atua as well. None of that was true for my connection with Alice, so I fidgeted uneasily on the chair.

"One of these days I'm going to hose her down with cold water, too," Alice told Dominic, and to my surprise, he smiled at her. A genuine smile that transformed his stern, handsome face into something breathtaking.

"I just might help you with that, human."

"I'll hold you to your word, saber tooth."

They nodded to each other, and Alice joined us at the table. It was like a twilight zone, the two of them getting along without hissing, snarling, and growling. My eyes narrowed on them, but they both had innocent looks plastered all over their faces. Dominic overdid it a smidge, giving away their debauchery. They were up to something, and I had every intention of figuring out what that was. Until I did, I'd be on high alert.

"Let's hear about all these smart things you want to talk about." Jabbing her elbows on the table, Alice cupped her jaw with both hands. "We are done talking stupidities."

I flinched.

Not that it wasn't deserved, but couldn't they cut me some slack. All of it was new to me. Doing everything as a group, speaking openly of my next move, worrying about someone else instead of just myself. *Kissing,* an uninvited voice chirped in my head. My jaw clenched, and a muscle started twitching under my left eye.

"She's losing her shit," Alice whispered loudly tilting her head toward Dominic, who was nodding thoughtfully.

"I can hear you," I deadpanned.

"I know," she piped in cheerfully.

"Okay, what in all the hells is going on here?" At my

words, Alice jumped from her chair, slapping both of her hands on the table with a loud smack.

"I want to tell her. Can I, cat?" She was shivering from excitement that freaked the hell out of me. "Pleeeaaseeee?"

"What are you, a child?" Dominic shook his head, but his mouth was curled at the corners. It had to be a dream. I was probably riding a high from the shifter's powerful blood. There was no other explanation. "Have at it, human. You will see that I was right." Folding his arms across his chest, he leaned back on the chair and made it groan.

"First, listen to everything without interrupting." Pushing the glasses up her nose, Alice turned to face me. She waited until I nodded warily before speaking. "So, since we know that you can make that jerk in the basement tell the truth when you use your juju on him, I had a great idea."

I was already hating whatever it was.

"You are going to wake him up again while saber tooth over here holds him as tight as a teenager grabbing his willy when jerking off for the first time," she continued. Dominic barked a laugh, but I was shaking my head, which made Alice talk faster. "That way he won't be able to move because I'll be down there too and using your blood. Since Dominic told me I could heal you by touching your blood, I'm going to try and do magic on him. Maybe we can force out whatever he can't tell us even with you making him say things, you know? It's a perfect plan, right?" All of it came out in a rush, making me blink fast to sort through the words.

Silence.

She wasn't even breathing.

"Absolutely not." My hand sliced the air, finality

resonating in my tone, and her face dropped. "Are you insane?" I rounded on Dominic. "You encourage this? What are you trying to do? Get her killed?" But he didn't even blink an eye at my outburst.

"I told you." He aimed that at Alice, who stuck her tongue out at him like a petulant child.

"He had nothing to do with it, Brooklyn." Moping, she plopped back on her chair. "This was my idea, and Dominic did tell me you'd be pissed. I just thought you had more faith in me, that's all."

It hurt.

I thought after she healed the wound, it made our friendship somehow more than what it was before that. Ridiculous to think that spoken words in any kind of exchange could tighten a connection, but there it was. And by denying her a very dangerous attempt, Alice thought that I had no faith in her or saw her as someone lesser than me. I wanted with everything in me to blame it on Dominic, but as I thought it, I knew it had nothing to do with the shifter. I just wanted to find someone else to blame instead of myself for once. With a sigh, I scrubbed a hand down my face.

"Alice." Searching her eyes, my throat tightened from the dejected look she was giving me. "This has nothing to do with my faith in you. When I said thank you and everything else after that, I truly meant it." Reaching out, I took her hand. She clenched her fingers for a moment before relaxing and wrapping them around mine. "What you are suggesting is not only dangerous if Johnathan is not restrained or somehow manages to make a grab at you…"

Alice frowned, but I could see that she was paying attention and not stubbornly sucking for no reason. My eyes flicked to Dominic, and he gave his consent for me to speak freely about what we discussed. Tightening my hand around hers, I took a deep breath.

"Dominic and I discussed this after you left the room to check on the wolf." I didn't care that the said wolf had his ears perked up and was listening to everything. If he dared repeat anything, I would remove the skeleton from his hide while he was still alive. "We don't think you are a witch, but we are certain of one thing. You are not fully human."

I expected her to either squeal in excitement or shriek while freaking out. She did none of it, just sat there scanning my face as if searching for deception. I waited for long moments before nudging her hand.

"Nothing to say?"

"I have a feeling that's not the reason why you don't want me to help with the dumbass from the basement."

"As a matter of fact, it has everything to do with it." I didn't know how to say it differently and not scare her, so I told her the simple truth. "We don't know what you could be if not a witch, but I can tell you one thing for sure. Although we've never come across someone like you, you are really powerful." Alice glanced from my face to Dominic, who nodded at her before turning her gaze back to me. "If we agree for you to do what you say and Johnathan somehow escapes his binds, the Syndicate will uproot this entire continent to capture you alive. If you think them hunting us is bad now, you haven't seen what the Council can do."

Alice shivered, the color draining from her face. The wolf surprised me by curling his upper lip and snarling while he pressed his side to her leg. Head tilted, I watched the mongrel. Either he truly bonded to Alice by some miracle, or he was a very good actor. I was waiting on the latter while opting on the former. He had protected her from the moment I saw him in her kennel. He almost died when we were attacked to assure that she was safe.

"That scum is not leaving this place alive," Dominic spat the words in disgust.

"I didn't say he was or that I want him to." I rolled my shoulders to relieve the tension there. I hated the fact that Dominic still jabbed here and there like he didn't trust me. It was exhausting. "All I'm saying is, what if? Are you willing to test that? Because I'm not. I know firsthand what happens to those deemed useful to the Council. I know my way around the cages like the back of my hand. Alice would not survive a day in the underground."

Dominic jerked back like I punched him when I mentioned the cages. His jaw was clenched so tight I thought it'd snap at any second. Rage burned in his eyes as he struggled to control his animal so he didn't shift. I had no idea why I openly spoke about it. It wasn't a conscious decision, the words just spilled from my lips because I wanted both of them to understand how serious what they heard was.

"Do you think he was telling the truth that Frederic can track him by his blood?" Dominic asked through clenched teeth.

My shoulder twitched in a shrug. "It could be. Alice made a valid point. If they fed me his blood too, it's all gone from my system. I'm willing to bleed Johnathan dry if you catch some game so we can give him enough blood for him to be able to speak."

"If we do that, do you think they won't come here again?" Alice was gnawing on her lower lip.

"It might take them longer to circle back that way

because they'll look for us elsewhere." A humorless smile stretched my lips. "But they'll be back. And when they do, I'll be ready for them this time around."

"A female with a plan." Dominic grinned, too. "I like it."

## Chapter Fourteen

"You really think this will work?"

Alice asked for the umpteenth time while I went up and down to the basement checking to make sure Johnathan was not drained to the point it'd take a week to bring him back. Dominic was holding a young deer high on his chest, while a tube was connected from its neck directly to the Atua's throat. My friend was standing at the trapdoor, waiting to corner whoever walked out because she had to know what was happening. I couldn't blame her; I'd want to know if I were in her shoes, too.

"I'm sure it will work," I assured her, taking her by the shoulder to move her away. The wolf trotted on her heels, plopping down as soon as she took a seat. "Are you doing okay?"

"I'm fine," Alice huffed, shoving her glasses up with her forefinger. "It's not me suckling on a deer." She chewed on her lip, and I bit back a smile.

"What is it?" It would take a few moments for Dominic to be done in the basement, so I figured I'd keep Alice talking. If I could get her mind off things, it would be less likely for her to get into trouble.

"When you said I'm not a witch ..." Trailing off, her teeth sawed over her lip on those words before continuing. "You also said I'm not fully human."

"I did, yes."

"What does that mean, Brooklyn?" Her gaze lifted from the top of the table where she was carving a line in the wood with her nail. "Am I going to sprout fur at any moment? Or am I going to grow pincers and jump one of you to chomp on your neck? Because let me tell you, from what I've seen so far, witch was the best-case scenario I was hoping for."

I had to bite hard on the inside of my mouth so I could keep my face expressionless. Alice was fascinated with my world, romanticizing it with whatever things she'd read in fiction books. I understood her need to belong, especially since she'd been stuck in the middle of a war with an army of monsters hell bent on killing us and just the three of us on her side, plus the wolf. The problem was, I couldn't be sure she understood the dangerous part of it. She was a fixer. That was Alice in a nutshell. If she saw someone hurting or struggling, she was jumping in headfirst to help. It was what got her in this mess in the first place.

"I am almost certain you will not sprout fur nor grow pincers, as you call them." Her eyes narrowed like she didn't believe me. "All we know is that you can do magic. Blood magic, to be precise, which would drain a witch in less than a minute according to Dominic, but it fed you energy after doing it for ten to fifteen minutes. That makes you ... not a witch."

"What, like a bloody witch?" I nearly laughed at the incredulous way she said that.

"Blood witch, you mean, and no. Those don't exist. I'm sure of that, at least."

She was bobbing her head absentmindedly. I could hear the gears in her brain turning from across the table. Racking my brain to steer the conversation in another direction, I remembered snippets of the nightmare I had on the train. Mulling it over, I couldn't see anything wrong with giving her something else to think about. Reaching behind my neck, I unclasped the necklace and brought it up between us. The stone dangled on the chain, making both of us follow the swinging with our eyes. Light reflected on the deep red stone from the electrical bulb above our heads.

"Are you trying to hypnotize me so I can tell you what I really am?" Alice snorted softly under her breath.

"If only it was that easy." My lips twitched at one corner, but I brought the stone down, laying it on the table and straightening the chain. "In my nightmare on the train, I was dreaming about ..."

"Veronica," Alice said at the same time as me.

"About a situation before the Council imprisoned her and about the night that she was killed in front of me." My throat tightened, but I pushed down the lump. "In my dream, she spoke more than what actually happened back then."

"What did she say?" Alice leaned forward, her eyes wide.

"In reality she said 'Love you, Bee' before she died. In my dream, she followed that with 'Figure out the pendant and you will find the truth. Look at the stone,' which could be just my imagination playing tricks on me, mind you. But it's been nagging me ever since."

Alice focused on the pendant with newfound interest. She didn't reach out to touch it, but she did bring her face so close to it her nose brushed over the surface of the stone. My attempt to occupy her mind with something else was a success, but for whatever reason, uneasiness clawed at my insides. Did I make a mistake by bringing Alice's attention to the pendant? Something inside me was screaming yes.

"It has some symbols on it," my friend muttered under her breath like she was talking to herself. "And I have a very strong urge to touch it." Her face lifted so she could look at me, her fingers gripping the sides of the table as if she was trying to strangle it. "I never wanted to do that while you were wearing it. I never even thought about it while it was around your neck."

"Don't touch it. I'll be right back." We both jumped when Dominic spoke.

The deer was no longer struggling in his arms, the creature almost sleepy hanging its head over Dominic's shoulder. He refused to kill an animal to feed Johnathan, and of course Alice suggested we could use the same method she applied the first time she fed me her blood. She was nothing if not creative with her ideas, which I had to admit helped us quite a few times in the last number of days while dealing with the Syndicate. Dominic returned before we had a chance to wonder why he wanted us to wait and stepped next to the table, looming over me.

"What do you feel when you look at it?" he aimed his question at Alice, watching her like a predator spotting prey.

I tensed.

"I want to touch it," she answered simply, unafraid of him. "Like I'm physically restraining myself from doing it, but I'm not sure I'll hold back much longer. My fingers are twitching for it." She wasn't lying. Both her hands were tucked under her legs.

"Touch it," Dominic encouraged. "But don't lift it off the table."

"Ummm, I'm not sure I can promise that." Alice twitched visibly, straining to hold back. I wanted to put the pendant back around my neck just to save her from the torment. I knew it was a bad idea, and I should've listened to my instincts. "I really, REALLY, want to touch it."

"Do you trust me, Alice?" As if using her name would make things better when asking a question like that.

"Yes," was her instant answer, while I shouted, "No" at the same time.

"Touch it." Dominic ignored me like I wasn't there.

Alice slapped her hand on the stone before I could snatch it from the table. Glaring at Dominic cost me, and hopefully it would be a lesson for another time. As soon as her fingers wrapped around the pendant, she gasped, and her eyes rolled to the back of her head. I jumped off the chair, or tried to, but Dominic barred me from reaching her with a tree trunk arm across my chest. When my friend's head snapped back, turning her face up toward the ceiling, I was ready to bite Dominic's arm off. I'd chew through his limb to help her.

"She's not hurting," he said it from the corner of his mouth, not taking his eyes off her. "Stop fighting me and look at her. She's not hurting, Brooklyn. Even the wolf is calm."

"Don't tell me what could happen when she touched it didn't faze you, you prick." I was fuming, although he did speak the truth about the mongrel. "That's why you stood here next to me, to prevent me from interfering."

"Is that what you think?" Finally, he faced me, and whatever emotion was brimming in those green irises was like a punch to the gut. "I'm standing here to stop you?"

My eyes darted around and over him, noting for the first time how he had placed a foot in front of me, which had me right at his back. Dominic was not trying to block me. He was actually in a perfect position to protect me if anyone attacked. Like Alice, for example. My mind glitched and repeated that a few times. Dominic was protecting me from Alice.

My human friend Alice.

"The two of you fight like a cat and a dog," Alice told us calmly, and both our heads snapped in her direction. "If you are done, can one of you please give me a pen and paper? I think I saw them in the living room at some point. If I go myself, I might not make it. I'm little dizzy."

"What happened?" I crouched next to her, elbowing the wolf when he got in my face, while Dominic went hunting for pen and paper. "Why are you dizzy?"

"It's not bad, Brooklyn. My head is spinning because I feel like I was sucked through a straw when I touched the stone." A smile started forming on her lips. "But I do remember the symbol that was etched above a cave." She beamed at me.

"A cave?" The blood in my veins turned into icicles.

"Yeah, a large cave, and the path led deep underground after you pass the symbol." Alice was getting back to her animated self, but I couldn't move.

Dominic cursing up a storm from behind me relayed exactly how I felt at that moment.

# Chapter Fifteen

"No."

"I'm not asking for permission, Dominic." Arms across my chest, I glowered at him.

"Good, because you're not getting it," he snapped back, blocking the hallway.

"Dude, never argue with a pissed-off woman." Alice was whisper-yelling advice to the stubborn shifter from behind me. "Even if she was human, the possibility that she'd bite you would be high."

"Maybe you don't know what that symbol means, but I do." The symbol Alice drew would've told me everything even if she didn't mention the cave. "My answers are there, and I'm not asking you to come with me. I go alone."

"How do you know that wasn't planted there to lure you back to the cages?" Something must've shown on my face because Dominic laughed with no humor. "It doesn't take much intelligence for a lowly shifter to know you've been there, Brooklyn. It wasn't your words that gave it away, either. It was your eyes. No one gets that look without staring death in the face more times than they can count."

"I don't think you are not intelligent." Okay, so I deflected the rest of what he said because I wasn't ready to open that can of worms. "Actually, I think you are too smart for your own good most of the time."

"He did make a good point," Alice chirped. "About the symbol being planted, I mean. I've never done that before, so I can't guarantee what I saw was some supernatural phenomenon. Look at Dominic, he turns into a huge panther for God's sake. How do we know there wasn't some magic juju slapped on the stone? Anything is possible now that you opened Pandora's box for me. If you tell me unicorns were singing Macarena and zombies had a "Say yes to the dress" show, I'd believe it."

Not just me, Dominic was eyeing her like she finally snapped from everything she had seen so far, as well. After she drew her vision, I asked them for some space so I could think about things. Instead of being a normal human and getting some rest or just waiting in another room, Alice convinced Dominic to help her protect the house. From the kitchen, I watched the grumpy shifter schlep bags of salt outside for her. Where she found so much of it was anyone's guess, but she took advantage of Dominic's strength and poured not one, but two circles of salt around the house, belching something about all evil and negative energy and entities to be forbidden from crossing over it. As if the more dramatic she made her voice sound, the better it'd work.

I didn't feel any magic stir the air when she did it, but I kept my mouth shut. If that wasn't bad enough, the two of them also dug out some old radio that Alice had been poking and prodding since, saying we could hear what was happening in Chicago while hiding here. The damn thing was dead, but she didn't give up. Even as I stared at her, she continued to turn the buttons on it, her ear cocked toward it. The wolf was perched next to her, keeping his narrowed eyes on me.

"I believe what she saw was true," Dominic said slowly as if too afraid to speak faster or louder. "But I don't think it's all of it."

"Should I touch it again, you think?" Alice perked up, forgetting about the broken radio.

"No," Dominic and I snapped at the same time.

"Geez. Easy killers. Don't say I didn't offer." Chin tucked in, her head wiggled strangely when she said it.

"Fix the radio, human." Dominic twitched before he was done talking, realizing it was a very bad idea.

"Oh yeah?" She shoved it away from her, sliding it to the edge of the table. "Why don't you fix it, cat? Or all you know how to do is talk shit just to piss me off. At least I'm trying to do something, unlike the two of you." She glared, but her glasses started sliding down her nose, which ruined the effect she was going for.

I watched Dominic to see his reaction, and that was the only reason I caught the movement before he ended up dead. A slight widening of my eyes was all it took for the shifter to twist around, turning his shoulders to the side and saving himself from being impaled by a set of claws. Johnathan's furious face came into view, and he snarled at us, fangs bared. I woke him after draining him to make sure he'd be able to drink the blood from the deer. It should've taken him longer to start moving, which made us complacent. That slight could cost us a life, or four.

Dominic shifted in an instant, a large feline taking his place. My ears started ringing when he roared, while I bolted to place myself between him and Alice. The wolf stepped to my side, and we both prepared to guard her. I knew Johnathan would come at me first. Hatred burned in his crazed gaze that took time to be earned. A black blur streaked from the side just as he hunched to pounce, and it barreled right at him. The shifter and the Atua rolled on the floor, jaws snapping and claws raking.

It didn't take long for Dominic to get the upper hand. Johnathan was weakened, after all, from being tied up and mostly out of it for long periods of time. My worst nightmare for the Atua to free himself around Alice came to pass, and the blood curdled in my veins. I wanted to help Dominic, but my feet wouldn't move away from her. Johnathan noticed that he would be bested, and as would be expected of a coward like him, he scrambled away from under the panther and darted for the front door. It was an actual entrance since the door was not fixed, leaving it open.

As soon as he was moving away from Alice, my feet unglued from the floor, and I bolted after him. If he escaped, we would have to move from the house and look for another place to hide. Dominic on my heels, we were stepping out through the threshold, our eyes locked on the Atua's back when the strangest thing so far happened.

Johnathan smacked into an invisible wall, and his limbs splayed in the air with so much strength the ground under my feet vibrated. The distant sound of a boom bounced in the air, and he slid down slowly, landing in a heap. He didn't move, and neither did we. Then Dominic shifted back, and both of us turned to look at Alice, who was right behind us with her hands folded over her mouth.

"I guess negative and evil entities can't just cross those lines in, they can't cross them out either," I told her, seeing my friend with whole new eyes. Eventually, I would learn to not underestimate her.

"It worked." Her voice was muffled through her hands. "Motherfucking sonofabitch, it worked." Glasses barely holding on at the tip of her nose, she turned her wide eyes from Johnathan's limp form to me. "Until I met you, I never knew I could do magic."

Dominic's head cocked to the side.

"You never felt anything strange, or some pull to try and do something?" Not trusting the kiss ass not to play possum, I headed to break his neck before he woke up. My ears were trained on what the shifter and Alice were talking about though.

"No," she whimpered when the snap of a breaking bone sounded in the front yard. "After I met her, I was getting the urge to buy crystals and light candles to set intentions, that sort of thing. But when you stayed at the kennel, I just knew I could do it. I felt it right here."

When I turned, she was pointing at the center of her chest. A shiver passed through me, which I ignored as I carried Johnathan inside. After dropping him off in the basement and wrapping the chain properly around him, I climbed back up to find them still standing at the front door, locked in a staring match.

"A Mimico," Dominic said to me.

"A what-a-wha?" Alice blurted, frowning at the shifter.

"A Mimico. That's what you are." He left her gaping at him to turn back to me. "I've heard of it, but I thought it was a myth."

"What is it?" He might've heard about it, but I had not.

"If they never come across someone with magic, they would live their entire lives as human, unaware of what they could do. But if they are in the proximity of a witch" — Those green orbs were looking pointedly at me— "they can mimic that witch a lot more powerfully than the original magic user. The longer the exposure, the stronger the Mimico. They were a powerful weapon from what I heard."

My eyelids lowered as if that would make all this crazy go away somehow. *This can't be happening; it cannot possibly be happening.* But it was, and I had to deal with it.

"Is that why I can hear it speak to me?" Alice whispered her question, and my eyes snapped open.

"You can also hear it?" She flinched at my tone. "Anything else you forgot to tell us, now is the time. Because no matter what you say, it can't get worse than this."

"That's all." My stomach twisted at the sadness on her face, but a sigh escaped me.

I only wished I stopped tempting fate to prove me wrong.

## Chapter Sixteen

"Where do you think you are going?" Alice jumped a foot of the ground when I snapped at her.

"Nowhere." Her eyes darted around. "I was just checking to make sure everything is okay. It is, so ..." She gave me two thumbs up with a strained smile on her face.

"Alice, stay away from Johnathan." Nudging her away from the trapdoor of the basement, I had to force her to take a seat. "He will only provoke you to do something silly, and you'll get hurt. Trust this as the truth; I've known him for a very long time."

"I just have this feeling that he might say something to me that he won't tell you." Shoving her glasses up, she chewed her lip. "It's just like ... I don't know, I just know it. Something not even your juju can make him say."

"I wish you would stop calling it that."

"And I wish you would stop treating me like a useless member of our group, yet here we are."

"I don't think you are useless." Cocking my head to the side, I examined her, and she kept avoiding my gaze. "Is that what you think?" Crouched down so she didn't need to crane her neck to look at me, I nudged her leg good-naturedly. "That you are useless in my eyes? Alice, you made the pendant come off my neck, something I never thought possible unless I was dead. And, may I remind you that you also healed me while providing an escape route and a safe place for us to hide. You are anything but useless, my friend."

"I didn't mean it that way. You know what I'm talking about." Her breath huffed as she crossed her arms over her chest. "It's always 'Alice hide, Alice run, Alice don't do that, Alice you'll get hurt,' and I'm tired of it."

"I only want to protect you." The defensive tone in my voice should've been indication enough, but it wasn't.

"Because of guilt," she hissed, and I jerked my eyebrows, raising them all the way to my hairline. "Don't look at me like that it's making me angrier. I know you, Brooklyn. While you're too busy killing anyone that breathes wrong in my direction, avoiding your feelings for Dominic and acting like a one-woman mission, I pay attention, unlike some people around here. You feel guilty for Veronica dying, for those assholes killing Dominic's family, and for me being involved in all of it." Her shaking finger pointed at my nose. "You think it's all your fault. Well, news-flash girl, it's not. So, how about that, huh?"

My chest was too tight, and all I could do was stare at her.

"It's. Not. Your. Fault." She pronounced each word slowly. "Just like me, Veronica was an adult capable of making her own decisions. And you didn't kill her or force me to come along. She could've stayed out of it, and I could've left you two when all this started, but I chose to stick around. Me. I made that choice myself, with my human monkey brain. Don't take credit for my actions."

"That is not what I am thinking—"

"Oh, no? And you don't feel like you need to pay the price for the jerks killing Dominic's family? It's not your fault, woman. I'll keep saying it until it gets through your thick, stubborn skull. You didn't kill them."

My ass hit the hard floor, which was thankfully cleared of all blood and gore after Alice put Dominic to work with a mop and a bucket. Lungs shriveled in my chest, I watched her face as she kept eye contact, unflinching in her statement. It wasn't like she didn't have a point. Guilt was one constant riding me hard through all of it. It startled me when she reached out and tucked some stray hairs that escaped my ponytail.

"If it's true that your mother was a witch, maybe that's why you have this fire red hair." Her forefinger was twisting the ends of my hair around it as she muttered it. At my inquiring look, she shrugged. "More books, but human lore is full of witches with red hair and green eyes. Just like yours, actually."

"That is why I need you to stay away from Johnathan and stick with Dominic." I figured the time was as good as any to tell her my plan. "I have to get inside the Syndicate and see what I can dig up about his claims. The shifter will protect you until I come back; he won't harm you."

"I'm not afraid of Dominic. He is all bark with no bite. He likes me, he just doesn't know it, yet." A smile tickled her mouth, but it was gone in an instant. "I don't think you should go there, but I won't be a hypocrite, so I'll keep my mouth shut. If anyone can do it, it's you lady Wonder Woman, Your Grace."

"What?" I could tell she was about to burst if I didn't let her say her peace.

"I don't need to ask you if you are telling Dominic where you're going because I know you aren't. I don't blame you because he is worse than you when it comes to others making their own decisions. Just …" I waved a hand to prompt her when she hesitated. "I think I should go down to see Johnathan before you go. It feels important that I do that."

"I see what is happening here." Gaze narrowed on her; my lips pressed in a firm line. "You were softening me up to get things your way. Is that it?"

"Did it work?" She arched an eyebrow, shamelessly grinning at me.

"I know I'm going to regret this." But she wasn't listening.

Alice was already up, jumping off the chair and bouncing on the balls of her feet. After a harsh clap, she rubbed her hands, smiling from ear to ear while I unfolded myself off the floor. I really needed to slink out before Dominic caught a whiff of what I was doing, and if allowing Alice to come down to the basement assured her helping with that, it was a good plan. As far as insane and dangerous ones go, at least, but beggars couldn't be choosers and all that.

"You are getting good at manipulation tactics," I told her. "Too good."

"I aim to please."

"It is not pleasing to me to be manipulated."

"You have a one-track mind, Brooklyn." She was vibrating from excitement as she moved along with me toward the trapdoor. "Protect. And everything else gets lost in the cracks. That's why you have me. I got that shit down pat and made it my bitch."

"The things you say sometimes." Shaking my head, I yanked the door open, ready to follow the stairs down, but she stopped me with a hand on my arm. I looked up at her from my crouch.

"Can you kind of stay on the stairs so he doesn't know you are there?"

"I need to wake him," I reminded her. "He will see me." She was gnawing on her lip again, so I waited.

"Dominic said I'm a Mimico."

"He doesn't know what he is talking about." But Alice waved me off.

Her chin jutted out in defiance as if daring me to contradict her. "If you give me some of your blood, maybe I can wake him? I'm not asking for a bucket, just a couple of drops," she rushed to assure me.

This was going from bad to worse.

Alice took what Dominic said to heart. It was amazing to see how she took pride in being labeled as something none of us knew anything about. We weren't even sure that what he said was what she actually was, yet my friend accepted it, and the fates help anyone who tried to take it away from her. For somebody like me who spent their entire existence being ashamed of who I was and the atrocities my kind had done, it was unfathomable.

I was already too deep in this insanity, so I figured what the hell? That was how we ended up with me plopped on my ass on the stairs with my head in my hands while I tried to pull my hair out, and Alice with her right palm, which was painted with my blood, extended in front of her like a holy grail in the basement next to Johnathan.

"All I have to do is scream." Alice said calmly, impressing me from inside the basement. I couldn't see her because the wall blocked my view. "And saber tooth will fillet you like a fish, so no monkey business."

"Come closer, human," Johnathan sneered, and my heart skipped a beat. "I promise I won't give you time to scream."

"How's your face doing?" She gloated, her tone making me close my eyes. "It was so much fun watching you get up close and personal with what this human can do. Don't you think?" She laughed in his face.

Who was this woman, and what did she do to Alice? I had every intention of blaming it all on Dominic. He was the one filling her head with magic and powers and shit. Tensed and strung like a bow ready to snap, I debated when to go snatch her and drag her out of the basement. Unfortunately for me, I needed her help to sidetrack the shifter, and her words from earlier were taunting me on repeat. If you asked me, not everyone should be allowed to make their own decisions. Alice being the perfect example.

"Don't lie, human, I can smell the deception on your skin." The Atua didn't believe his own words. "You are not a witch."

"I'm not." Those two words were loaded with so much meaning it gave not just Johnathan but me a pause, as well. "But I'm not here to talk about me, dude. I have a couple of questions for you."

"And what makes you think I'm going to tell you anything?"

"The way I see it, you can tell me on your own, or I can make you. I'm not Brooklyn, but I have my own ways. I'll leave that part up to you. Tick tock, your time is up. What's it gonna be?"

My lips started curling from the way she talked, all cocky and confident, until magic prickled my skin, drenching me in dread. I scrambled off the stairs, plastering my body to the wall so I could poke my head out a little to see what in the fates name was happening. Thankfully, Johnathan was gaping at Alice or he would've seen me with my mouth open, too. My friend was standing just out of reach in front of the Atua, her right hand where she smeared my blood raised flat between them. Tendrils of red and black magic swirled from her palm like baby snakes hungrily snapping for their first meal. All the short hairs on my body were up at attention. I couldn't see Alice's face, but I felt her awe as if it was my own.

"It cannot be." Johnathan breathed, his face draining of all color. The magic reflected in the dark color of his irises, curdling my blood.

"Guess again, fucker." Alice leaned toward him, and I received another shock when he jerked back so violently, he almost toppled over with the chair. "You will tell me what I want to know, capisce?"

Her answer was frantic nodding, much to my dismay.

"Is Brooklyn's mom still alive, or did you lie about that?"

"How do you—" Johnathan started.

"Answer me," Alice shouted, jabbing her palm closer to his face.

"From what I've heard, she is alive. I cannot say for certain because I have not seen her."

"But they say she is alive, correct?"

"Yes."

"Who are they?"

"The Council."

My fingers ached where I was clinging to the wall, which was the only thing keeping me standing. I forgot how to breathe, blink, or think. Alice was firing questions like a drill sergeant, and Johnathan was answering on autopilot, staring unblinkingly at her palm. I'd seen witches do their magic, but nothing like I was witnessing in this basement. Obviously, Johnathan must've since I'd never seen him so afraid in my life.

"How about her dad? Is he alive?"

"No, he is dead. Again, I cannot be sure because it's only what I've heard."

"So, he could be alive, too?"

"Yes."

"How did he die?" The question passed through me with a jolt. I never thought to ask how my father died. I believed the stories I was told about him. It was the only solid truth I had.

"The Council killed him."

Alice gasped as my knees gave out, and I dropped hard at the bottom of the stairs. The world tilted under my feet, and everything was spinning uncontrollably. *No, no, no, no,* a voice was shrieking inside my head. It can't be. They had his portrait looming over them in their chamber. Why would any psychopath kill someone and then tell stories of braveries and honor, holding that person in such high regard that every Atua wanted to be just like him. My father died protecting the Council, protecting the Syndicate. I had to believe that. It was the truth.

Wasn't it?

"Why would they kill him?" My friend's voice sounded distant until Johnathan spoke, and his words snapped every-thing back into focus.

"Because he loved a witch more than his own kind," the Atua spat the words like a curse. "And they created a freak like her that should have never existed." Johnathan's dark eyes were shooting daggers at me when I locked my gaze on his. "The Council has killed any hybrid that has ever been born, apart from her. Not from lack of trying."

The cages, the pain, the never-ending drifting through agony in an abyss threatening to devour my soul … it all crushed me, pressing me to the cement floor. Johnathan laughed with insanity visible in every line of his face.

"The bitch just won't die. So, they used her, and instead, they killed everything and everyone she cared about. She will be their weapon and under their thumb, or she'll be nothing at all. They'll destroy countries to get to her." His sneering face tilted toward Alice. "And now, it'll be your turn. You and that dumb fuck I can feel standing at the top of the stairs. Both of you are about to die."

"No, you're about to die, you piece of shit," Alice hissed.

I felt Dominic too, but I couldn't look away from Johnathan. Not even when Alice screamed and slapped her hand with the swirling magic on his face. The Atua's roars of agony echoed for a very long time, matching the anguish suffocating me. I didn't care.

I felt empty.

Numb.

# Chapter Seventeen

"At the first inkling of trouble—" Dominic started for the umpteenth time.

"I'll start taking my clothes off and slow dancing," I deadpanned, but he didn't look impressed. "I'll get the hell out. Yeah, you told me."

"The human is rubbing off on you."

"Please don't tell her that. I'm having enough trouble convincing her she's not an X-man." Dominic arched a brow. "Her words, not mine. It's all movie or book references with her. Apparently, that's how her brain can process things."

"Humans are strange creatures."

We were crouched on top of a warehouse in downtown Chicago, Dominic's thigh and arm brushing mine as we waited. The lights of the city were casting blue, yellow, and red hues on everything, an occasional honk or hoot from a passing car piercing the night. The stench of stale water, wet asphalt, and petrol permeated the air, clogging my nostrils. A chain-link fence rattled in the blast of wind that slapped my ponytail around my face. The deep bark of a dog punctuated my sentiments.

I felt like barking, too.

Barking and biting.

"You filled her head with Mimico, or did you forget." Talking to him was a good distraction or I would curl up in a ball and never get up. "Next, we'll be chasing her across the city when she decides it's time to dash out her own brand of justice. I hope you are aware of that."

"Reminds you of someone we know?" He snickered when I glared at him, that damn dimple blinking at me.

"That wolf better do what he was told." In my attempt to get some distance between us so I didn't feel his body touching mine, my foot kicked a pebble. The sound ricocheted on the roof like a bullet, and we held our breath, but the Guardians we were scouting never looked up. "The last thing we needed was Alice popping out of nowhere. I couldn't deal with that right now."

"He will."

"What's his deal anyway?" My head stuck out over the edge of the roof, flicking fast to assess the situation. The two Guardians were still talking to the person shrouded in shadows at the mouth of an alley separating the warehouse and an impound lot filled with vehicles in all shapes and sizes. "Why does he stay in his animal form? Is there something wrong with him?"

"It happens at times of high distress or trauma." He tugged me back when I hung over the edge for longer than he liked. "Our animal tries to protect us, and until we are okay, it'll stay in control."

"I wish I had an animal to take my place when I needed a break from life," I muttered begrudgingly.

"You still feel everything." A smile ghosted over his full

mouth, which I found fascinating for some dumb reason. I jerked my gaze away with effort. "We just do it on four legs instead of two."

"How sure are you that this talisman will do its job and I'll get inside undetected?" My fingers dipped in the pocket of my pants and curled around the wooden disc etched with runes on both sides.

"It will do its job," was all he gave me.

"You ever going to share how you make deals with witches when the Syndicate is the only place I've seen them? I know the Council has them on a tight leash, so there's no way you can get to them. Unless—"

"Let it be, Brooklyn." He scanned the city around us as I watched his profile. "I'll tell you one day, maybe. For now, just trust it'll help you."

"Unless someone in the Council is helping you." I finished my thought, but he said nothing, his mouth set in a tight line.

"They are on the move."

I leaned forward to see the person in the shadows had disappeared, leaving the two Guardians alone at the mouth of the alley. After Alice got information I didn't want from Johnathan, I had to fess up to Dominic that I planned to get inside the mansion and snoop around. He didn't stop me, but he tagged along no matter how much I argued about it. At least Alice stayed behind where she would be somewhat safe. That was why Dominic was with me, and he would stay outside. If a large group of Atua were headed in any direction, he would follow them. That way he would get Alice out if that was their destination.

We didn't have to worry about Johnathan. He wasn't dead, per se, but he wasn't alive, either. Whatever magic Alice conjured in her hand melted the skin and bone on

his face to the point of no recognition, but the rest of his body was intact. There was no heartbeat either, yet I felt his power, though it was faint enough to have to hunt for it. So, we left him in the basement after Dominic pounded a metal hook in the ceiling—with his fist of all things—and he draped Johnathan on it to dangle like a carcass from the metal chain. We waited for anyone to exit the mansion so I could sneak in when they returned. The wards around it would drop to allow the Atua entrance, and no one would be the wiser that I got inside, too. It was a solid plan.

In theory.

Just as I turned to move away and leave him behind, Dominic took a fistful of my shirt and yanked me to him. His mouth crushed mine, unyielding and demanding. I gasped, and he took advantage, his tongue invading my mouth. It twirled around mine aggressively as he wrapped the fingers of one hand in my hair. My own arms snaked around his neck, and I clung to him while he devoured me. Nose full of his scent, I was swimming in a sea of need the likes of which I'd never felt before. We shared breath until he slowed, releasing my tingling lips and pressing his forehead to mine.

"At the first sign of trouble, you get out." Voice raw and raspy, he was breathing hard as he yanked on my hair to drive his point home. "Say it, Brooklyn."

"I'll get out at the first sign of trouble," I repeated after clearing my throat, although I still sounded breathless. Those swollen lips were taunting me, too close and yet too far away. "I have to go."

"I don't want you to go." I stilled because I knew how much it cost him to voice his feelings.

I will be back before you know I'm gone. I promise."

Neither the shifter nor I believed that, but we were both good at pretending.

Forehead still pressed on mine, those green eyes stabbed me to my soul. Dominic allowed me to see all the fear, apprehension, and dread that was going through his head, and it was crippling to witness. This powerful male that stood up fearlessly to the Syndicate was worried about me. Not long ago, he'd threatened my life, and every second word coming out of his mouth had been a jab aimed at what I was. Did he finally see beyond that into *who* I was instead of what? And what did that mean? That just like Alice, he saw some quality that could redeem what Atua had done to the rest of the world? There was too much I wanted to say, so much I wanted to ask, but I only brushed my lips softly across his and moved away from him before he could stop me. Because he did want to prevent me from leaving that roof, and I could see it written all over his handsome face.

With one hand on the edge of the roof, I vaulted over it, sailing through the air and dropping in the shadow-filled alley in a crouch. A dumpster sat halfway open, and the odor wafting off it was strong enough to peel paint off the walls. Despite all that, when I straightened, my fingers raised to my lips, which were still stinging from Dominic's kiss, and I couldn't help but smile. Maybe there was a light at the end of this tunnel of unending darkness for me. As I sauntered out of the alley like I owned the city, I could've sworn that I saw that light blink. It was just a small wink, but it was there. All I had to do was walk through the Infernal Regions without being burned and reach it.

Right after I was done dealing with the Syndicate, that was.

# Chapter Eighteen

I caught up to the Guardians just as they waited for the tall iron gates to swing open and allow them access. Sharp pointed peaks jutted from the gates, glinting in the moonlight like the open jaws of a monstrous beast waiting for its next meal. Both large males stepped aside for a limousine to drive through, and I ducked between two bushes, hunkering down so I wouldn't be noticed. The long black vehicle slowed, and the back window cracked open an inch, but I couldn't see crap from the leaves stabbing me in the face. If I made too much noise, I had no doubt they'd come to investigate, so I waited, although it killed me because I wanted to know who was inside it.

"It is arranged," one of the Guardians grumbled, his voice so harsh and deep you'd think he'd been chewing razor blades daily instead of gum.

The limo drove off, the red lights fading until they disappeared in the distance. The two goons stomped up the long driveway, and the gates glided in, resembling the wings of a black swan curling in on themselves. I waited until the last moment, and when the opening was just wide enough for me to slip through, I did.

Manicured lawns with topiaries stretched in front of me, clustered close enough to provide cover, and I darted deeper on the property. As long as no one actually laid eyes on me, they would never know I was prancing around among them. From experience, I knew my power and energy registered as Atua. Any Atua. So, unless I gave them reason to investigate, I should be okay.

The night was approaching an end, and grey streaks were already lightening the sky. It was the best time to prowl inside the Syndicate's grounds since all of them would be taking a rest soon. Some Guardians would stand watch beside the witches and humans, and I was counting on that. Those, I could deal with. With that in mind, I took a wide turn around the mansion and squatted near one of the walls, watchful for any patrol.

This plan would only work well and wouldn't backfire on me if they acted in character. The Council was arrogant. They prided themselves on the power they held, so never in a million years would they expect me to pop in for a visit. As far as they were concerned, I would be running for my life, praying to never see any of them again. I would not be coming to share breakfast while they were hunting me like an animal. When I couldn't wait anymore, I stood up, cracked my bones, which were stiff from being tucked in a corner like a mouse, and looked up the three-story wall that loomed above me.

Unsheathing my claws, I sunk them in between bricks and started the slow climb up. I had to pause here and there when a corner broke off and rolled down, or when a sound made my ears perk up. No patrol came around, and no window was cracked open. When I reached the roof, I sprawled on the tiles, releasing my breath. The easy part was done. I flipped around and very carefully crawled around until I found the small door nestled between the rooftiles. When it wouldn't budge, I raised my fist and crashed through it before darting to the side where I waited to see if someone would come to see what the commotion was.

No one came.

Before long, my legs dangled down, and holding my weight up with just the tips of my fingers, I soundlessly dropped in the middle of a hallway on the top floor. The only floor where no guards would be lining the walls and where no one dared come uninvited. The Council's bed chambers. The rest of the large mansion would be brimming with activity. I knew this because my own room—the one I used to have—was one floor below. The squeal of a hinge from a door opening had me diving to the side and plastering myself to the wall in the best impersonation of wallpaper that I could muster. A knock brushed against wood somewhere ahead of where I was playing a spider on the wall.

"If you have come to apologize, I do not wish to hear it." Isaiah's voice drifted to my ears before a door slammed closed. The rapid tapping of knuckles followed it. "Go away." That time, I felt the vibration through the wall I was hugging when the door slammed with a loud clap.

Curiosity had me inching sideways, gliding closer to see who decided to disturb Isaiah when the ancient fool wanted sleep. When Frederic's platinum head came into view, the blood in my veins curdled. Bare chested, the Council member had a silk robe hanging from his shoulders and billowing behind him as he stormed away from Isaiah's door. Silk sleeping pants were sitting low on his hips, and he padded over the thick, red carpet barefoot. A storm was brewing in his gaze, and his face was pinched in anger. The only thing that hid me from him was a tall half column with the large, golden bust of a naked woman perched on it. Frozen in place, only my eyes darted around in search of an escape route in case he noticed me.

That was when the third door came into view.

Well, the edge of it since it was behind me. In my curiosity, I didn't pay attention to the other side of the hall. I was very grateful neither Alice nor Dominic could see it. I'd never hear the end of it. The only reason I was on the third floor of the Council home was because I had a feeling if they wanted to hide anything, that was the place. No one could enter without them knowing about it. No one apart from me, it seemed. Lurking around to avoid everyone paid off sometimes. That was how I knew about the small door on the roof. When I didn't hear Frederic enter his chambers, my gaze snapped to where I last saw him. He was standing with one hand on the carved doorknob with his eyes narrowed at the bust of the woman hiding me.

My heart jumped to the roof of my mouth and stuck there.

"What's with all the snapping?" Samir spoke from right behind me before his door was even opened, the soft light from his bedroom falling on me like a spotlight. My eyes squeezed shut, waiting for both of them to jump me.

"Never mind," Frederic snarled and entered his room, slamming the door shut.

Very slowly, I unplastered myself from where I was hugging the wall and turned to face Samir. Just like Frederic, he was wearing silk sleep pants that hung low on his hips, but no robe. Leaning one meaty shoulder on the doorframe and arms crossed over his bare chest, he watched me, humor twinkling in his chocolate brown eyes. He straightened and gallantly waved his hand, inviting me in.

I gulped.

Why didn't he tell Frederic that I was right there between them? And what was it with the fucking smiling and polite invitations? The longer I glared the higher the chance he would alert the rest. Just as I would've attacked and gone for his throat, Frederic's door opened. Before my brain registered what was happening, Samir had me pinned on the wall, his face tucked in my neck.

"Take it to your chambers, Samir. We don't need to hear you slobbering all day." Frederic sneered and slammed the door again.

"Move with me, he is still there." Samir's words were just a breath over my skin. A shout lodged in my throat when he picked me up, and the next second, he was closing his own door. My mouth opened, but he slapped a hand over it, tapping the back of my head on the wood. "Go rest your old bones Frederic, unless you want to join us?"

A soft click punched the air from my lungs.

"You should not have come here." All humor gone, Samir smoothed a hand over his goatee. "Sit."

His chamber was not what I expected. Jewel-colored silks were draped over rods on each window. Low side tables with a lantern perched on each were sprinkled around the large space between colorful pillows thrown all over the floor. Round tables sat clustered here and there, filled with crystal glasses and ice buckets with Champaign bottles sticking out of them. Dark shutters were blocking the daylight from the room, and the dancing flames of the lanterns reflected on the glass of the windows. Instead of a king-sized bed, there was a huge pillow fit for a T-Rex on one end of the room, with white gauze like waterfall around it.

Where was I supposed to sit exactly? I might be idiotic at times, but he would never say I was dumb. Opting to stand, I crossed my arms. too.

"So much like your father, child." Samir cracked a smile, shaking his head. "And what did you think you'd accomplish by coming here, might I ask?" He kept his voice low enough that there was no way anyone could hear us outside of his chamber.

"My mother is alive," I spat the accusation at him with as much venom as I could. Since he caught me, I had nothing to lose. An arched eyebrow was all I got for the effort. "And you killed my father, too."

"Ah, well that is not exactly the truth, but I see you are learning things that should've been left buried. Technically, I did not kill your father." He didn't even bother denying anything else. My blood was boiling. That was when he delivered the bomb that almost knocked me on my ass. "I should've known Dominic would be too lenient with you. That boy is a pushover, and you are too hot-headed," Samir said with a grimace.

"You are the one helping Dominic?" I hissed after I was done gaping like a fish.

"Quiet." Samir bared his fangs at me, his eyes locked on the door and his head cocked as if he was listening to something only he could hear.

"You are lying."

"Yet you still breathe, child." The disappointed look he gave me set my teeth on edge. After a long moment of silence where we stared at each other, he threw both hands in the air in frustration. "You do not think that boy saved you the night Veronica died without help?"

I racked my brain for what he was saying. That cursed night, along with the nightmare I had on the train, swirled behind my eyes, and then clarity hit me like a punch to the gut. *I couldn't breathe. Someone was screaming. It was a broken and loud sound. A window shattered to the side, the glass falling like rain over the tiles and making chiming noises as if it was music to accompany the mournful cry. A sharp pain in my throat as my vocal cords ripped told me it was me screaming.*

*Everything seemed surreal.*

*So, when the sound of fighting echoed above me, I didn't think anything of it. Nor did I blink an eye when my curled-up form was lifted off the floor and I was wrapped in two strong arms that for some stupid reason made me feel safe instead of afraid for my life. I think I heard Samir's voice say, "Get her out of here," but that couldn't be the truth.* My gaze locked on the Council member.

"Why?" I knew at that moment that he did speak the truth. I thought I imagined it that night, but it was him. It was Samir's voice I heard talking to Dominic.

"I gave my word to protect you." Samir flinched when I arched an eyebrow that called him a liar. I'd like to know where his protection was while I was in the cages, but I kept my mouth shut. "I had to keep up pretenses, and I might've made mistakes, Brooklyn. But I kept my word. As I said earlier, you breathe."

"Gee, thanks." My life turned into a giant rabbit hole that was getting wider the deeper I got inside it. Insanity threatened at the edges of my mind. "Do me a favor and try not to protect me. I might have a better stab at life." Dropping on the nearest pillow, I stretched out, tucking both hands behind my head. "Now what?"

"Now we should get you out of here."

"I'm not going anywhere until I find something that will tell me where to look for my mother."

"Brooklyn, you need to leave that be. If you stir up that horrible mess, your father would've died for nothing. What you need—"

"Don't tell me what I need. I know what I need, and that's answers. Where is she?" No longer calm, I curled my knees up, hugging them to my chest so I didn't strangle him. Not that I could do it, but I was willing to give it my all.

"I do not know." With a sigh, he plopped down next to me. Since he wasn't trying to impress the other two fools, he looked almost normal. And much younger, especially after he stabbed his fingers through his hair, mussing it up. "Your father died and took that information with him."

"You talk about him like he meant something to you."

"He was my friend, Brooklyn." The ghost of a smile tickled his mouth, but it was gone before it formed. "I was there that day. When you were born."

"You were obviously there the day he died, too." Unwilling to let emotions screw with my head and turn me into a dumbass, as was proven by Johnathan, I clenched my jaw. "What stopped you from helping him? You were scared to break a nail? Is that it?"

"You know nothing," he snarled at me, but I was past the point of being afraid of him. If he wanted me dead, I would've been out in that hallway. "Isaiah and Frederic were too strong to be bested. I fought with him, but we just couldn't win that battle. They had help. They offered him lenience if he told them where your mother was. He chose death. They offered me my place on the council if I kept my mouth shut, so I agreed. Don't look at me that way. Your father was already dead, and being one of the Council was the perfect position to make sure you lived."

"You said they had help. From who?"

"You are your father's daughter." Samir beamed at me

proudly, and all of a sudden there was not enough air in the room for me to breathe. "The witches helped them take down your father."

"We will get back to the witches. What do you mean take him down? Take him down from what?" Braced for another bomb, I kept my unblinking gaze on him in case he tried lying.

"With help from the witches, Isaiah and Frederic, planted false memories on a large scale, Brooklyn. Half of the witches died after performing that spell because their lifeforce was too drained to keep them in the land of the living." Samir was getting comfy on his own pillow, and the entire thing struck me as very odd.

Then the truth slapped me upside the head.

"You were expecting me." He handed me a crystal flute that he filled with dark liquid. I smacked it out of his hand. It spilled all over his sleeping pants and both our pillows. "You wanted me here so you could tell your side of the story."

"And you are as smart as your mother." Samir saluted me with his own glass, chugging it down in one gulp. "Let us hope you're just as cunning."

That didn't sound ominous at all.

# Chapter Nineteen

"No wonder Dominic didn't lose his shit when I said I'd be coming here." Samir chuckled at my grumbling.

"He did send a word telling me to watch for your safety." Pretending to pour another drink, he eyed me sideways. I made a note to ask the shifter when he had the time to send word and how. "I believed he was doing me a favor by keeping you safe. I'm starting to see I might have been mistaken." My face turning red was all the confirmation he needed, so he just offered a nod.

"You were saying?" My hand circled in front of his face impatiently. "Get back on the subject. This was not a social call."

"Alright, alright. Let me see …" He lifted his gaze to the ceiling, and his irises glossed over. "It was a very long time ago," Samir muttered, more to himself than me.

"It couldn't be that long, Samir. I'm not as ancient as you, or did you forget that part?"

"Ah, thank you." He waved off the confusion clouding my face. "The witches cast the spell to hide a few things

Isaiah and Frederic didn't want anyone else to remember. Only the four of us knew the truth."

"Four? You mean my father was the fourth one?"

"No, your father was dead when the spell was cast. Noah was the fourth one. I believe you met him the night of the attack, no?"

Met him? I fought that dipshit when he waved my father's dagger in my face. To Samir, I gave a dip of my chin only. I'd wait to see what he had to tell me before I spilled everything I knew. I still couldn't wrap my mind around the development of him and Dominic working together.

"The spell." The reminder was countered by a narrowed look on his face.

"The spell was cast after they killed your father, so no one could contradict what they set into motion. Before then, there was no council, Brooklyn. There was no Syndicate."

"What are you saying, Samir? Can you just spit it out? It's freaking me out."

"Your father led the Atua as the only leader, Brooklyn. Those were the good days for our kind. I used to be his advisor and closest friend. But Isaiah, Frederic, and Noah were with us too. He never saw them plotting against him. Neither did I, for that matter."

I was too stunned to do anything but stare open-mouthed.

"You must never repeat this to anyone, child. If they catch an inkling that you know, nothing will stop them from getting their hands on you. They cast the spell making everyone believe the Syndicate has always been our way and that the Council ruled from the beginning. In reality, it's been only a few centuries. After your father's death."

"So, my memories are altered too? Because it doesn't feel to me like I've been alive that long."

"That was the strangest part." Samir gulped another glass in one swallow, already refilling it. A jolt passed through me when I noticed his hand trembling. "Before he died, your father made me promise to keep you safe, and he told me not to look for you. When the time was right, you would be delivered on my doorstep."

"This is ridiculous." A throbbing headache was developing behind my eyes.

"It is the truth." With a sigh, he scrubbed a hand over his face, and every day of his ancient life was visible in his gaze. "It was decades that I waited, and just when I thought you must be dead as well and was ready to give up, a knock on my door brought me face to face with you. A small youngling wrapped in a blanket dropped outside my door. This door to be precise."

"I don't understand. Didn't you say decades?" I was getting sick to my stomach and hoped I wouldn't hurl all over Samir.

"Yes, decades, yet you looked just like the day you were born. I saw you that day and gave you my blood, too. A gift so you could call on me if you ever needed my aid." He searched my face, but I had no idea if he found what he was looking for. "I never questioned why you hadn't grown as if you were locked in time only to be delivered to me later. Knowing your mother, nothing would surprise me. She was the most powerful witch I had ever seen. If anyone could make you suspended in time, it would be her."

"And?"

"I couldn't hide who you were the more you grew. Isaiah and Frederic are many things, but fools they are not. You look too much like your mother. There is no mistaking that red hair and those eyes. So, after killing you failed, they tried breaking you so you could be used as their weapon. Even as a child, you were as stubborn as you father. You never did anything you didn't want. I tried protecting you as best I could, agreeing for your memories to be altered, pretending I was working with them … all was well until Johnathan got involved."

"That's how I ended up in the cages." My gut twisted.

"I rejoiced when you ended up in the cages." I jerked back at the hiss that came from him.

"What in all the hells, Samir?"

"They sent that idiot to get close to you, not to just spy and tell them your secrets, you stupid child. They couldn't break you and use you as a weapon. So, they sent him to seduce you. If they couldn't have your powers at their whim, they could always train your child as their puppet. I didn't kill that useless male only because his greed made sure he ran to Isaiah and Frederic to rat you out, so he was not able to be alone with you outside these walls. You being in the cages made sure he couldn't get anywhere near you. There, I kept you alive while I employed Veronica's help. If they wanted to play games, I could do it too."

Mind spinning, I sagged into the pillow. What Samir was saying destroyed the last shreds of reality inside me. Were any of my memories the truth? Did every person I thought of as a friend act as such because they were told to do it? Weight pressed on my chest, and numbness spread through my limbs. What was the truth? In the fog clouding everything, one thing he said stood out.

"It was you. Every time they would bleed me dry in the cages, you came to feed me so you could keep me alive." It wasn't a question, and he didn't answer. He only watched me steadily. A hollow laugh passed my lips. "To what end, Samir? What's in it for you?"

"I gave your father my word." He looked offended, but I had a nagging feeling there was more to it.

I waited.

"If you knew your mother, you'd keep your word too," he finally muttered, eying me sideways. That time I accepted the flute he offered me. I'd drink poison at that point.

"So, from what I gather, they killed my father so they could rule, for power. They wanted to use me because I have magic in my blood. What I don't get is why all the rest of the bullshit. Casting spells, erasing and altering memories. That makes no sense to me."

"That's because you don't know the history of our kind. No one does after that cursed spell, and let me tell you one thing: Isaiah and Frederic will bury both of us alive if a word gets out about this." Samir was leaning so close I could smell the coppery taste of the blood he'd been drinking on his lips.

"The witches and the Atua were mortal enemies. Before your father met your mother, we were thinning in number and falling like flies. But she loved him, you see. Together, they made a pact, and for the first time, we had peace. It didn't suit everyone, especially those having a gain from the war, so a group of the witches made a different deal with Isaiah and Frederic. The witches never expected to be tricked. After that spell when half of them perished, the rest were imprisoned, and to this day they serve as the Syndicates' puppets."

"But we are stronger and more powerful than the witches." As the words spilled from my mouth, the thought about

Alice and everything she'd done so far made me falter in my conviction.

"Only because they are cut off from half of their magic," Samir confirmed my suspicions. "When your father was killed, your mother placed that curse on them."

"On the entire witch kind?" That was not possible. No one was that powerful.

"They called her the Keykeeper. She was … is the vessel that filters the connection of raw magic and the witch kind. They killed the one she loved, and she slammed the door in their face. If she ever appears and decides to open it again? Many in this building will be praying for death that will never come. Especially after she hears what they have been doing to her daughter."

A shiver ghosted up my spine, pebbling my skin.

"We are on our own, Samir." I had no idea why I said it. "If my mother was alive, she would've showed her face by now."

"Not yet." He glanced around as if expecting someone to be spying now after everything else he said without care in the world. "Before she does come and show herself, a few things need to happen. First, your father's dagger that she made for him must appear." My heart dropped at my feet, and the said dagger burned through the fabric of my pants where it was strapped to my thigh.

"What's so special about that dagger?" I asked offhandedly, hoping he wouldn't notice I was strung as a bow.

"It never misses. It's etched with sigils, and it'll always find its target. Only your bloodline could heal from a wound of that weapon. Anyone else would die." I had a bad feeling gathering in the pit of my stomach.

"Is that the only thing that needs to happen for her to come out from wherever she is?"

"A mortal enemy needs to freely offer his blood to an Atua without expecting anything in return." My body did visibly flinch with that. Dominic offering his neck and later watching me as I drank from his wrist played in front of my eyes.

"Is that all?' I croaked, and Samir was eyeing me strangely, but I couldn't care less.

"A mage needs to appear." When I stared at him blankly, he shrugged, twisting his mouth in distaste. "It's a witch but not a witch. It could only mimic magic." My heart was kicking like a wild horse against my ribs at that moment, leaving bruises internally, no doubt. "They called it a mage, A Mimico. Although I think that one is a myth." He breathed the last parts under his nose, frowning at the flute in his hand. "Anyway, when a mage forms a bond with an Atua, a soul bond, your mother should come."

Feeling my friend's awe as she watched the tendrils dance in her palm was playing on repeat in my head, and I tilted to the side when dizziness swept over me. Alice. He was talking about Alice, and if that bond was not fully formed, it was only a matter of time. What would my mother do to someone that is not a witch but can mimic her magic? And she hears what happened to her daughter after they killed the male she loved. If everything Samir said was the truth, there was no one more powerful than her when it came to magic.

No one but a Mimico.

No one but Alice.

Fuck.

# Chapter Twenty

Before I could say anything, the door to Samir's chamber burst open, splintering into small, sharp pieces that stabbed at my skin. I was stuck in a loop inside my head, freaking out about my mother, and not even seeing Frederic's murderous face could shake me out of it. The funny thing was, I couldn't care less if my mother decided to pop into the world of the living. Up until the point where my brain registered that she could see Alice as a potential threat that needed to be removed, I was all for it. After that, a few things became clear.

First thing, my mother loved my father, and she had every right to hold an eternal grudge. Hell, I'd help her torture and kill the assholes. But nowhere in that picture did anything confirm how she felt about me. In her right mind, she had me frozen in time, only to drop me off in the Council's hands. The more I thought about it, the more convinced I was that I was making the right decision. Between my mother and Alice, I'd pick Alice any time.

Second thing, Samir couldn't find out about my friend.

Or how chummy Dominic and I had become. He gave his word to my father, and he was keeping it because he was shitless scared of my mother. I didn't factor anywhere on that scale. You guessed again, I'd pick Dominic and Alice any time.

Third thing, Frederic and Isaiah were useless pieces of shit that needed manipulation to keep their power. I had seen the hatred in some of the witches down underground when they had to do what they were told. It also became clear why they couldn't stand to look at me. My mother cut off their magic, and there I was, waving my hair like a red flag in front of an enraged bull. Again, no thank you, I'd pick Dominic and Alice any time.

That left one thing.

I had to get the hell out of the mansion because Frederic was ready to rip me apart limb from limb, Isaiah right behind him. Samir and I were on our feet, and he stepped forward, placing himself between them and me. Their expressions told me they'd heard, if not all, at least some of our conversation. But I didn't need Samir's help, so when he barreled into the other two, I followed on his heels.

Jutting my elbow up, I caught Frederic under his chin, and his head snapped back as we toppled down and tumbled over the carpet in the hallway. I snapped my fangs a hairsbreadth from his face, and he kicked me in the stomach, sending me crashing into the opposite wall. I rolled back to my feet, stayed crouched, and searched for a way around him. I had to go back to my friends and tell them everything. They had the right to know what kind of fresh hell was coming our way before it was too late. Unfortunately, windows were a no-go with all the damn shutters blocking the way. Unless …

My body jerked to the right, but I moved left and away

from the brawl happening in front of Samir's door. No witches or Guardians were there, but it was just a matter of time. Frederic, the idiot, bought my trick and went flying face-first into the column, holding the naked bust of a woman. The statue wobbled and then dropped over the back of his head with a hollow thump that made me cringe. He stayed down long enough for me to reach the shutter-blocked window at the end of the hall. Samir had Isaiah pinned under him, straddling his chest.

I slapped my hand on the button, poking out on the right side of the window, and with a low hum, the shutters started rolling up. Heart jackhammering my ribs, I watched Isaiah claw at Samir's chest, opening deep gashes. For just a second, I considered jumping out and leaving him in the hallway to fend for himself. It didn't sit well with me, so as soon as daylight spilled through the half-open shutters, I turned my face away and shattered the glass with my elbow. Shards stabbed through the fabric of my shirt, but I ignored them.

"Samir," I called out, already crawling out the window. "Let's go, I will not wait for you." I heard his thumping footsteps as I dropped three floors down.

He landed next to me a second later, and we made a mad dash across the manicured lawns. Shouts followed us, and bullets whizzed past our heads, but we didn't slow. The daylight made us slower, but so much adrenaline was pumping through my veins that I felt like I was flying. Samir kept pace, although his bare chest was bathed in blood.

Weaving through topiaries and hedged bushes, we were halfway to the tall metal gates when Guardians rushed to intercept us head on. Samir and I split in different directions, hoping they would follow just one of us. As I anticipated, they all gunned in my direction. I saw Samir taking a wide turn and darting my way from behind them. That slowed my running feet until I stopped, planting my hands on my hips.

I smirked at them.

On a whim, I reached back and unclasped the pendant from around my neck. Without taking my eyes off their stunned faces, I tucked it in my pocket. My mouth opened to talk smack to them just to piss them off when I felt it. It was like my feet were stuck to the dirt ground and it was slowly seeping my energy. What in the hell? Luckily, the Guardians were too stunned by my pendant removal they didn't attack straight away. My eyes locked on Samir, and a rock dropped in my stomach. The guilt was there, written all over his face. All his words from the time he found me in the hallway came assaulting my brain.

"She didn't cut half of their magic," I hissed at him. "She cut all of it. They are sucking everyone here dry to be able to use magic." I felt like I was about to vomit.

Samir didn't deny it, he just nodded once.

"Fuck you," I spat at all of them and darted toward the gates.

Samir caught up with me, but I ignored him, too angry to even look at him. We pushed our way to the two iron gates and almost got decapitated when a sword came at our necks out of nowhere. Samir shoved my shoulder and made me stumble, taking the tip of the blade in his hand. It cut into his palm, and blood gushed like a waterfall to the ground. He didn't release it until a black blur catapulted over the gates, casting a shadow over us. The large black feline dropped directly on the Guardian holding the hilt of the sword and crushed him to the ground. Bones broken, he stayed crumpled, unable to move. Green eyes locked on me, and they flicked up and down, scanning for injuries. I took a lesson from Alice.

I rolled my eyes.

The panther roared and barreled into the iron gates, bending the bars so bad a small person could squeeze through the gap. The shifter moved back before repeating it twice more and made a hole big enough that we all rushed through it. Dominic apparently decided to take the lead, and we followed without a complaint. At the first chance, we started weaving between buildings, over chain link fences, and through alleys. The Syndicate was on our heels through the city.

Two Guardians blocked out the exit at the mouth of one alley. Dominic pounced on one of them, and I tugged the dagger from my thigh and slashed at the second. Samir's sharp intake of breath told me he knew which weapon I had in my hand, but that was his problem. I wanted to get away from these assholes. We would've too if tires didn't screech and a silver sedan didn't come to a stop on the side of the street. Alice rolled the window down and was frantically waving us in. The wolf was glowering on the passenger seat. I saw the moment the Guardians made the connection. Either me or Alice would get out of the city that day, but not both.

"Samir, you better help him get me out of there," I told him, and he froze next to me. Grateful that Dominic was already loping toward Alice because he knew I'd freak out if she wasn't protected, I locked eyes with my father's best friend. "Tell Dominic everything, word for word, what you told me, and make sure he doesn't get hurt when he comes after me. Give me your word."

"I give you my word, Brooklyn." He hesitated. "I could

go." It was ridiculous for him to trade places with me. They' never go for it.

"Make sure my friends are safe." And just because I could, I smirked at him. "Or I might tell my mother when she comes that you didn't exactly stick to your word." When his jaw dropped open, I laughed only so I didn't start crying.

I was already dreading all the pain I would receive. With a wink at Samir to mask my fear, I sashayed out of the alley on the street. Alice was smiling at me, and a lump formed in my throat. I heard the vehicle's screeching tires moving our way just as Dominic squeezed his large feline body in the car with Alice. Samir was there next, and without warning, he plucked Alice from the driver's seat, dumping her next to the wolf. His foot was on the gas before the door closed, and I dropped on my knees, placing both hands at the back of my head. The furious cry of a large feline shriveled my bone marrow, and I watched the back windshield burst into shards. Dominic tried to squeeze out, but he was too big to fit through it. I'd counted on that. His wild eyes locked on me, and a tear trickled down my face. The Guardians surrounded me, but I held his gaze.

"Come for me," I mouthed, and he roared.

My head jerked, and the crunch of bone filled my ears before darkness swallowed me.

Those piercing green eyes followed me into the abyss.

# Next in the Infernal Regions for the Unprepared Series

vinci-books.com/everlastingfire

**An undead heart bleeds when struck by the right weapon.**

Brooklyn's bloodlust clouds her judgment, but Dominic seeks a cure while risking everything. Can her best friend bring Brooklyn back, or will they all fall into darkness?

Turn the page for a free preview…

# Everlasting Fire: Chapter One

Life was all about cycles.

Ups and downs of a rollercoaster ride where the only way to survive is to buckle up and hold on tight.

Or, scream your head off.

I truly believed that I knew that, but it always took one more kick in the kidneys that buckled your knees to drive the point home. On a good note, when the knees hit the ground there was no other option left but to go up.

I kept telling myself that.

One day, I might believe it, too.

Forearms resting on my raised knees, I watched the metal bars of the cage with dispassionate detachment of a lost soul. Was I lost? No, definitely not. At that point I had more things I cared about—people that counted on me—to simply give up. I still owed it to myself to stay adrift if only just for a while, and finally face everything I'd discovered and all that was taken from me.

The strangest thing in it all, something that kept

returning in my mind, was that the one place which haunted my every nightmare, or waking hour, didn't affect me as expected. Maybe I should've said not as bitingly as I thought it would. The terror was there, deep in my psyche like an insistent insect prodding, buzzing.

I simply ignored it because if I focused on it, it would've driven me insane.

Clammy skin and a quickened heartbeat along with the shivers crawling up and down my spine served as a reminder of my predicament. The cages were not a place anyone would easily forget. Not even an Atua. But, the thought of Alice and Dominic out there alone and targets for my enemies was more frightening.

Samir better make good on his word and look after them.

I knew I was too good of a prize for the Syndicate to pass when I surrendered so the rest could get away. Foolishly, I told the shifter to come for me. It sounded smart at the time when I said it because all I wanted was to send him away and keep him alive.

As I sat in the cramped space between the metal bars, I realized my mistake.

"I never thought I'd see you here again," a familiar voice rasped from somewhere in the darkness. The harsh whisper was too loud for the silence around us. "I should've known you'd be back. No one leaves this place for long."

After a few years, I had thought I'd never see the hell hole again, but I didn't vocalize my rebuttal. The voice succeeded in reminding me that you never truly left this place. The rancid stench of body odor, dried—or fresh—blood along with the moist soil squelching under the feet of the patrolling witches, was permanently absorbed in our skins to torment our every waking hour. My eyes adjusted way too easily to the barely visible stone walls, embracing the dull light which was hardly above the flicker of a dying candle. The memory fed on our fear like a leech sucking the life out of us.

I'd used that voice many times as an anchor to ground myself to life while I struggled to stay awake, bleeding all over the packed dirt. It whispered tales of worlds and people that didn't exist, just to torment me more and force me to stay alive. In those times I loathed it and was grateful for it, too. I never remembered the words, but the tone? I'd recognize that tone anywhere.

"Nostalgia." My shoulder rolled in a blasé shrug while I picked on my chipped nail. "They made me feel so at home here, I was starting to feel sentimental for the familiar stench as a free person out in the world." The voice hummed part in disbelief, part in amusement. "No one wants to see me all sappy, or slobbering all-over the place, so I had to come back. Me crying is a horrible sight, believe you me."

"You should've done everything to stay away. Things have changed down here from the last time we spoke. The witches are dying," the person whispered dejectedly, but before I could ask more questions it fell silent. I felt the person distancing themselves like a physical push to the chest.

For so many years, I heard the voice cajoling me to hold on, to not give up, yet I never saw the face it belonged to. I thought they didn't want to be alone and in some twisted sentimentality did everything to prolong my suffering by talking until I opened my eyes. They were in a cage just like me because I heard the clinking of the metal bars every time the person shifted, yet I had no idea if it was a male or a female. To me, it was just a raw rasp, a tone that never allowed me to find peace in death. Only the darkness prevented me from coming face to face with my tormentor and savior.

It was nice to see the Syndicate gave me back my old cage though. How very thoughtful of them. At a closer inspection, I did recognize the tiny space which had been my home for too long. The scratches left in the hard-packed dirt where I sat were also familiar. I left them there while I was writhing in pain on many occasions.

"Someone's comin'," the voice hissed.

That was when I heard the scuff of shoes on the ground. Soft, but not nearly silent enough for my next-door neighbor or me. My shoulders tensed as I subconsciously reached for the dagger on my thigh, finding an empty sheath. I curled my fingers next to my leg and stared ahead, acting as if nothing was amiss.

"You truly are a sight to behold, Brooklyn." Frederic emerged from the dark void as a dim light bloomed into existence from behind him.

Eyelashes fluttering, I blinked rapidly from the sudden light in the pitch black of the space until I brought him into view. His long hair was falling loose around his shoulders, the platinum color turned orange from the torch flickering behind his head. Ominous shadows were cast over his high cheekbones that made his eyes look sunken into his skull and his perfect face resemble an angel of death. Dressed in an immaculate suit, the Council member stood out like a sore thumb in the pits of hell he created for the rest of us. My gaze dropped to my feet so he couldn't see the hatred burning there.

"The service is impeccable here, as always." Keeping my voice light, I smiled coquettishly at the ground, but he saw it. Frederic missed nothing. Rage was coming off him in waves, strong enough that it was difficult to breathe. "The care they offer makes me glow from the inside. I'm assuming I have you to thank for that, Sire?" Calling any of them Sire bubbled acid up my throat, one I had to swallow down.

"I will take great pleasure in breaking you." There was nothing remotely humane in his promise. Which was loaded with anticipation, judging by the slight tremor in his voice. "I didn't have nearly enough fun the last time you were here."

"I'm looking forward to that." My eyes slowly lifted so I could peer at him through my lashes. He had enough self-preservation to take a step back when my lips curled and the smile turned wicked. The reaction pleased me immensely which made him livid. "Should we start now?" I purred.

Frederic moved so fast I had no time to twist away from his grasp. The magic the witches had woven into the bars of the cages sapped my strength until I was as good as a human in a fight against him while surrounded by the metal bars. He took hold of the collar of my shirt in his fist and yanked me hard against the metal, mushing my face between the bars.

"You think you can stand against me, child?" His breath washed over me when he got in my face. "Just because I like toying with you, it made you think you can win against me?" My body shuddered in revulsion when his tongue poked out and he licked a trail up my cheek. "It's been too long since I've had your blood." The murmur shriveled my veins because I was sure I wasn't meant to hear it.

It brought memories of fangs ripping into my arms and thighs as I was too busy being delirious while my life flashed and flickered in front of my eyes.

So many times.

Too many…

"I wouldn't dream of it." My words were muffled by the cage biting into my skin, but I had to keep him talking. If he decided to feed, there was no way for me to get away without tearing my neck open. "Only a fool would dare think they stood a chance against you."

"Precisely." Shoving me away as if I disgusted him, he glowered down his nose at me when I slumped on the dirt. Stroking their egos worked no matter the situation. "Now, let us talk about our dear friend Samir."

Crawling on my hands and knees, I tucked myself in the narrow cage as far away from his reach as possible. My reaction earned me a chuckle that I wanted to punch from his face. Unfortunately, my prison was only tall enough to sit in and just wide enough to move a couple of feet to the left and right, which meant I had to wait for my chance. I'd been shoved here for a few days already, and my muscles were sore from lack of movement. It was crazy to hope they forgot about me, yet I did, until this ass showed up.

"What about him?" Keeping my eyes locked on his, I wiped the cheek he licked with a grimace. "You miss him already?"

"What did he tell you?" He folded his hands at the small of his back before flaring his nostrils. "And don't lie to me, girl. If you don't tell me the truth, your life means nothing to me."

"He said I'm the most beautiful Atua in existence, and he has been secretly in love with me my whole life." My eyelashes fluttered as I coyly curled my lips. "Can you believe it?"

Angering Frederic was a dumb idea.

It didn't stop me from doing it, but I found it necessary

to acknowledge the fact even if it was just to myself. My kind could smell a lie. Well, the more powerful of us could, but my experience in the pits of hell taught me how to bypass it somewhat. I might have been inexperienced in the matters of the heart thanks to Johnathan and his betrayal, but I wasn't an idiot. I knew Dominic liked me, so I kept the way he looked at me when he thought I wasn't paying attention firmly in mind as the lies spilled from my lips.

Frederic frowned disapprovingly at me.

"You lie." He spat it like a curse, and even the witch holding the torch behind him flinched. Luckily for me, doubt was riding his tone hard.

"Am I though?" Tilting my head to the side, I focused on the witch.

The male had the hood of the robe lying flat on his shoulders, exposing his face to me. Sunken cheeks formed dark shadows on it over the sigils swirling there, but his shrewd eyes were tracking my every word. Back when I spent all my days in this place I feared those like him. Now, with the information I had, I had to wonder if I could recruit their help.

On its own my hand lifted, reaching for the pendant that was no longer there, but I caught myself in time. Spearing my fingers through the clumps of unbrushed hair I tugged on the strands to untangle them. Let Frederic think I was vain, as long as he kept his hands and fangs to himself.

"It's astounding. You really think you will survive this a second time." Unease prickled the back of my mind at the delighted glint in his irises, but I pressed my mouth shut. Crouching down so we were at eye level, he cocked his head, the long strands of his hair spilling over his shoulder. "Tell me, Brooklyn. How far do you think I need to go until you break? We already know the limits that will bring you to the edge. All I need to do is push just a little when you are there."

"To what end?" I was truly curious. "What makes you think I'll be of any use to the Council if I'm broken? I might turn on you at the end."

"Ah, but you already did turn on us, did you not?" He traced one of the bars with a fingertip while eyeing me as a lion would eye a bloody steak. "For that, you must be punished."

It wouldn't be the first time and I knew his punishments well enough. There was something in the way he said it though that sent a shiver through me. Years of pretending not to be bothered by their insanity and depraved ways served me well to keep my heartbeat calm, but my mind was a different matter. My mouth formed words I had no reason voicing out loud.

"Punished how? What is it you think you can do that you haven't done before?" His growing smile chilled me to the bone.

"I wonder if the shifter would enjoy watching me feed on you." The fangs grew longer as he spoke, and my heart stilled in my chest. "Do you think it'll please him if I do it from your neck, or from your thigh." His gaze raked over me, pausing over my breasts and my pelvis although it was hidden from him with my curled-up legs.

"I'd definitely try the thigh, if I were you." The witch sucked in an audible breath at my answer. Even Frederic's eyes widened at that. "I bet that will rile the shifter up like nothing ever would."

"We shall see." His eyes flashed with eagerness as he stood and strolled away, taking the light with him.

I breathed a sigh of relief.

Dominic was too smart to be caught by the Council, I

had to believe that. But if the worst happened and they brought him to the cages? Taunting Frederic that I was looking forward to feeding him from my thigh was the smartest way of getting Dominic and me out of the hell hole. Because for Frederic to reach my thigh…

He had to unlock the cage.

## Everlasting Fire: Chapter Two

"Get up." The bars of the cage rattled as something smacked hard against them, and I gasped as I woke.

The magic keeping me contained must've forced sleep on me because the last thing I remembered was taunting Frederic. After he left, I stewed in my anger, thinking of all the ways I wanted to slice him up the first chance I had my hands on him. Rubbing the sleep away, I squinted at the flickering flame on the other side of my prison and the witch glowering impatiently at me.

"Put these on." Metal clanked and jangled at my feet when he threw something at me.

Twisting around, I reached for it, only to end up dangling shackles from my fingers. Sigils were painted on them and I didn't need to ask to know they'd keep me docile when outside the cage. In the face of my reality, white noise filled my ears.

"I don't think so." I threw them back at the witch.

"Put. Them. On." He snarled each word and hit me on

the cheekbone the second time he flung them through the metal bars.

The side of my face smarted, but I bared my fangs at the ass. "Why don't you unlock the cage and come put them on me yourself?" My fingers itched for the dagger, but I curled them into fists.

"You are only making things harder for yourself." His huff told me I was acting childish. I disagreed.

"Look around you." My hand flopped to the side, pointing at the darkness and everything I couldn't see in it. "It doesn't get harder than this."

"Put them on, I just need to deliver you to the Gulley. We will both be punished if I don't." He waited with a furrowed brow. You'd think speaking to me like to another living being was a foreign concept.

My heartbeat stuttered.

Faint memories tried to push to the front of my mind but no matter how hard I tried I couldn't recall them clearly. My time at the cages was fuzzy in details but made up for it with dread and terror every time I closed my eyes. At the mention of the Gulley, my skin became soaked in cold sweat and my hands begun to tremble.

I searched his narrow face but didn't detect a lie. Without my abilities I wouldn't leave this cage if it was anyone from the Council, but the witch was not that big of a threat by any stretch. I might not be as fast or as strong with my powers muted, but I had fangs. No magic could take those away from me. If the witch tried anything, I'd just rip his throat out.

Gingerly, I picked up the metal and secured it around my wrists.

The door of the cage clinked open the second I was bound, and it swung outward with an ominous shriek of a dying dinosaur in the quiet. The witch smoothly stepped aside and waved his hand for me to crawl out of it, which I did with a lot of muttering under my breath. My muscles were screaming when I unfolded to my full height from the lack of proper circulation, and I stumbled into him. The male steadied me with a firm grip on my arm but didn't protest otherwise as I expected him to do. It allowed me to prod for information while I had a chance.

"What's at the Gulley?" Keeping my tone conversational, I rubbernecked to see if I'd notice something familiar in anything that was revealed from the flickering torch he clutched like a lifeline.

"Death," he told me gloomily.

Whimpers, soft cries, and sniffles were like ghostly whispers haunting everything around us. The stench of wet soil, old congealed blood, and excrements drenched the air and made it pungent enough to be tasted on the tongue. I breathed through the mouth so I didn't empty the contents of my caved in belly and didn't dignify his answer with a comment.

Of course it was death. What else would the Syndicate have hidden in the underbelly of the city. The scuffing of my boots over the packed dirt just drilled it home better. I chose to think of the people that got away and were safe somewhere instead of what was waiting for me. The Council had me to entertain themselves, so maybe they'd leave them alone now. Unfortunately, Samir was with the two I wanted to protect and that made my hopes only wishful thinking.

Any witty comments I had for the witch felt unnecessary.

We reached a tall wooden door after what felt like forever, but I had some exercise so I didn't complain.

Docilely, I stepped to the side and waited for the male to unlock it. It opened to another barred door. That one clanked and screeched loudly as he pushed it inward before he nudged me with the back of his hand to enter it. The moment I stepped through, it slammed shut at my back, pushing me to whirl around on the witch who stayed on the other side of it.

"Give me your wrists through the bars," he ordered, his gaze darting around. "And try to stay alive for a while longer. Don't make them risk everything just to find you dead."

I narrowed my eyes but did as he said, and with a wave of his hand, the shackles fell to the ground. We stared at each other as I memorized his face. Unlike most of the male witches who were bold enough to display the sigil tattoos all over their skin, he had extremely short but still visible dark hair. Most noteworthy, however, was the strange color of his eyes. They were so light green it was almost like looking at shards of glass, not irises of a living being. The male was a bit more muscular compared to the rest, but I couldn't tell if my assessment of that was true because of the flowy robe he had draped over his shoulders.

My body came alive now that the suppressing magic was gone, so I had no time to say anything when he scooped the shackles up and closed the wooden door in my face. Alone, I rolled my shoulders and turned in a small circle, wondering what to do. It was a long hallway with a faint light at the end and nothing else. Moist stone surrounded me and the stench of moss assaulted my nostrils.

At least my abilities were back.

Whatever this place was there was no magic around it apart from the metal door. Pointing my feet toward the faint light, I cautiously headed in that direction. My fingers wiggled in the pocket of my pants, and I breathed a sigh of relief when they brushed against the pendant. In the cage, I didn't know who was watching, so although I could feel the stone there, I didn't dare check.

"Here she is." Frederic's voice set my teeth on edge the moment I entered the illuminated area.

Excited murmurs reached my ears, and blinking rapidly, I brought the vast space into focus. Dread filled me in a tidal wave, and I wished I could unsee it. Atua filled the space around the room above my head, all of them leaning hungrily down to see me better. Isiah and Frederic were lounging on throne-like chairs in the middle of them, dressed to perfection while I stood at the edge of what appeared to be an arena.

My fists clenched. "Why am I here?" My voice boomed and bounced off the high ceiling.

"To earn your keep." Frederic grinned at me with a sadistic jubilation and waved at someone I couldn't see.

All my senses became alert when a ferocious cry of a beast blasted my eardrums a second before a furious creature joined me from the opposite side of the flat dirt. My lungs shriveled when it rose on its hind legs and shook its head. I wanted to say I'd never seen anything like it, but the memories my mind normally hid from me said otherwise. At least two heads taller than me, the creature could've passed for a wolf in another life. What stood a few yards from me was a wolf ripped in half and the two parts were connected by a humanoid form—as if a human grew inside the beast and ran out of space so it split it in half while it continued to expand.

Pitch black eyes with no pupils locked on me, and it roared so loudly the ground under my feet shook violently enough to make me stumble. Its jaw, as long as my arm, was opened wide enough that I saw its tonsils.

Dread petrified me, and I stiffened.

The packed dirt trembled when the beast ran for me. First on two legs then it dropped and loped toward me on all four. Instinct took over and my muscles loosened as I placed all my weight on the balls of my feet.

I waited, my eyes locked on the monster drooling for my blood.

All the noise dwindled in the back of my mind, and I could hear everything about the creature. Each thump of its heart, every scrape of the claws when it pushed off the ground, the breath sawing in and out of an elongated snout. Nothing but me and the creature existed.

It pounced from a few feet away. Just as it was about to snap razor-sharp teeth on me, I ducked and rolled away under its belly to jump back up on my feet behind it.

My own claws and fangs burst out.

The beast shrieked an outraged cry as it smacked hard into the metal bars and skidded to a stop. I didn't wait that time and with a running start jumped on its back. My claws sunk into its shoulders, but my attempt to rip its head, or the throat at the very least, failed. Thick fur filled my mouth, my fangs closing around it with no purchase.

A scream was torn from my chest when it reached back and shredded the skin on my arm and shoulder with five-inch claws. Its massive upper body swung frantically as it attempted to shake me off, but I dug my own fingers further in and squeezed my thighs around its torso. When I was certain I wasn't going to be flung like a dirty rag, I pulled one arm back behind me and, angling it right, I stabbed the claws in its side. They slid smoothly in the human-like skin, and it shrieked a second before black blood gushed from the wound.

Atua were hooting and cheering around us, their joy like acid burning my insides. The moment of losing focus cost me. Tipping to the side so I could reach the skin instead of fur didn't give me as good of a leverage as I hoped. The beast twisted unnaturally around and plucked me off its back like I weighed nothing. I scrambled to grab a hold of its arm, but my blood coated hand slipped over the fur and the creature pitched me to the side.

I sailed high and managed to turn in the air just in time to hit the ground on my hands and knees instead of my back or head. The impact jarred my bones, and I bit on the side of my tongue, filling my mouth with my own blood. One of my fangs pierced my lower lip, and I snarled in pain. Packed soil rattled under my palms when the beast thundered over it to reach me. I had no time to stand up, so I stayed kneeling in front of it.

Putrid breath like decayed flesh slapped me in the face as its jaw opened wide. The creature was about to literally bite my head off, and my own roar of fury mixed with its insane roar of victory. At the last minute I made my move. My hands snatched the open jaw in a bruising grip, and adding everything in me, I yanked in the opposite direction, placing all my body weight into it.

The breaking of bone and tearing of muscle was too loud in the deathly silent arena. Hot blood sprayed me from head to knees and the scream of the beast died down so suddenly it made my ears ring. Gasping for breath and trying not to vomit, I let the broken jaw of the creature fall off my limp fingers and searched the crowd for Frederic and Isiah.

I locked my gaze on them through the blood dripping down my face.

"Impressive." Isiah's slow clap echoed around the large space in the silence, but all I could see was him tearing out Veronica's heart.

Panting, I rose to my feet. "Is that all you've got?" I already heard the second beast snarling from the other side of the arena.

Arrogantly arching one eyebrow he brushed silky hair over his shoulder with elegant fingers. "I'm just getting started, Brooklyn. So eager to die, just like your friend. I'm very pleased." Frederic chuckled next to him like the mention of Veronica amused him.

"You are just getting started?" Repeating the question made them smile indulgently at me.

I grinned back.

"So am I."

With that, I brushed all thought about the second creature away and sprinted for the wall separating the Council members from the arena.

Grab your copy…
**vinci-books.com/everlastingfire**

## About the Author

Maya Daniels, USA Today Bestselling and multi-award-winning supernatural suspense author, is a fun-loving woman with many talents.

She traveled the world, gaining life experiences that helped her career as an investigative journalist, as well as her storytelling. Maya writes compelling tales of magic, mythical creatures, loyalty, and life-changing friendships with snarky female characters—much like herself.

Her travels have taken her to Europe, Africa, Asia, Australia, and America. Born with her feet in motion, she currently resides in Ohio, spinning her next epic story that you will not want to put down.

Her biggest 'sins' are her love of chocolate and coffee—through an IV drip! One to never sit still, Maya practices Reiki healing, different types of martial arts, reads about the arcane, talks to furry creatures more than humans, picks up a sledgehammer for home improvement, and travels with her fated mate, seeking her own adventures.